in tHis is Love

RUBEN CHAVIRA

ISBN 1-4116-5384-X

7 DUCKLINGS PUBLISHING

Cover/Layout Design © PhDesign – *Peter Hanegraaf*

in tHis is Love

To Derlings
1 John 4:10
From Your Papa

Rubeul Hawke

CONTENTS

CHAPTER ONE

~~~

In The Beginning…

SAMUEL CRUE TOOK ONE LONG LAST LOOK AT HIMSELF in the full-length mirror on the dressing room door. This morning he was especially glad that he had finally hung the mirror for Stephanie. She had asked him to hang a mirror on the dressing room door for years. He had finally got around to putting one up. He and Stephanie went together to get a mirror. It took them an entire day to find the right one. Another day to get it hung on the door just right. Once it was hung it was well worth the effort. Stephanie loved it. Particularly on those occasions when she felt that she had to look especially nice. She would spend several minutes making last minute adjustments to her hair and clothes. Those special adjustments that were noticeable only to another woman. Or to a husband. And he always noticed. He was always proud of the way she looked. Always the Lady. Always lovely. Always beautiful. He was glad he had hung it for her. Especially today. It was one of those occasions when he felt that he had to look especially nice.

A little self consciously, thinking he looked somewhat like Stefy at that moment, he made some last minute adjustments to his uniform. He made sure that the alignment between his fly, belt and shirtfront were centered. His military alignment he called it, left over from his Marine Corps days.

He still remembered his drill instructors pounding it in. The edge of the shirtfront had to be exactly aligned with the fly on his trousers. Then the right edge of the belt buckle had to be aligned with both. Somehow that subtle practice seemed to make a world of difference in his appearance. He never forgot it.

He made sure that the top edge of his tie clasp was aligned with the line formed by the top edge of his shirt pockets. Next he checked to see that his nameplate was straight and centered exactly 1/4 inch above the right breast pocket. Finally, he examined the placement of his badge, which hung proudly over his left breast pocket. He noticed the badge, seemingly for the first time.

Across the top it read, CHIEF, in bold royal blue letters. Chief. He was the Chief of Police. How had that happened? He still remembered clearly all of the days and nights he had spent in a patrol car or on footbeat. He remembered the years working nights and graveyard shifts. The cold that invaded his bones during winter nights spent checking alarm calls or standing in the pouring rain, trying to make sense of a simple traffic accident. Then came his first promotion, to Detective. He remembered all of the days he labored over a stack of cases assigned to him as a robbery detective. He remembered the names and the faces as if they were yesterday. So many years ago. Then came more promotions, more assignments and now he was Chief. How had he risen to the top? When had all of that happened? The grace of God was all he could attribute it to.

Now today, his son was graduating from the police academy. 28 years after he himself had graduated from the same academy. Following his daddy's footsteps, as he had followed in his fathers footsteps. He remembered his father, the gleam in his eye, the puffed up chest, upon his graduation from the academy. "Sgt. Crue's son is graduating from the academy tomorrow," they all said the day before the graduation. The whole station was abuzz with it just as it had been yesterday. "Chief Crue's son is graduating from the academy tomorrow."

Samuel Crue thought of his son. How he would soon be working the streets. It was a different day he thought. A different job than when he first started. More violence, less respect for the badge. It was a tougher job now. You had to really want it. You had to have a special love for the people, those you were sworn to serve. Oh, he knew there were guys who were in it for the ego, the power of the badge, the chance to carry a gun. But today more than ever, you had to want it for the right reasons. Otherwise, it would turn out all wrong. You'd wind up in the newspapers. Silently, he prayed for his son. He prayed for the police department. He prayed for police the world over.

Samuel took one last look in the mirror. He was ready.

"Sammy," she called. "Are you coming or do I have come up and dress you myself." No one called him that, Sammy, except for Stephanie. It sounded funny. But when she called it, it was filled with love.

"Coming, Stefy," he answered. "I was just admiring myself in that mirror of yours."

"Oh, you and that dratted uniform," she teased. "Like a little boy playing at cops and robbers." He started down the stairs and saw her standing at the bottom looking up at him, with that look in her eyes. The same look she had when he first saw her 25 years ago. He had been in uniform then, too. He had been 23 then. Two years on the job. She had been 21. Slender. The tinge of a tan on skin as clear and smooth as silk. Her hair a rich brown, streaked with strands of gold, hanging past her shoulders with just the hint of a curl. The eyes a deep, clear brown. Her teeth as perfect and white as a string of pearls set by the finest jewelers. And that look. It had never gone away. Neither had her beauty. The years had just refined it.

"You look wonderful, Chief," she said. "But let's go. The graduation starts in one half-hour. It would not be proper for the Chief to be late."

Samuel looked at his watch and saw that it was 8:30. She was right. Time to go. He walked down the stairs and wrapped his arms around Stephanie. She leaned against him and laid her head against his chest. "So, what do you think of your son now, ma'am," he said, one hand gently stroking her back.

Stephanie sighed and scolded, "You men. Of all the things in this world that you could choose to do for a living, what do you do? You choose to put yourselves in danger. It wasn't easy putting that boy through college. He could have been a doctor, anything!"

"He would have been good at anything, too," Samuel said.

"I guess I always knew he would follow in your footsteps," Stephanie added, feigning disappointment. "I always knew that one day he would have to go out and save the world. From the day he was born I knew. And the things you've taught that boy. Honestly. Sometimes I think you love the people more than you love me."

She leaned her head back and looked up at Samuel, "And he is his fathers son, isn't he?"

He winked at Stephanie, releasing her from his grip. He said, "It takes a lot of love to do this today. It always has, but today more so that ever. And I do love them. Sometimes I think they are like poor lost sheep, without a shepherd. And there are plenty of two legged wolves out there preying on them. Can you imagine what it would be like if there weren't men like our son around, willing to risk their own lives to see them safely home."

They paused awhile thinking about it. Stephanie shuddered at the thought. More so because, now, her own son would be out there fighting the wolves.

Samuel looked at his watch, folded his right arm, offering it to her and said, "Your chariot awaits my lady." She smiled, took his arm and they walked, side-by-side, heading for the door. They paused at the door gently holding hands while Samuel prayed for their safety and for God's direction and blessing on their son and his new profession. Then they headed out of the door, arm in arm.

CHAPTER TWO

How You Are Fallen From Heaven...

"COME ON, DAD," LUCIUS WARD PLEADED AS HE PUT down his travel bag. "It's spring break. Everybody's going. All I need is three hundred dollars. Make it two. Just two hundred dollars. That's all I need."

Lucius was a tall, gangly 19 year old, a year out of high school. His hair, though not long, was unkempt, falling over his ears and into his eyes. His oversized clothing, consisting mainly of T-shirts and jeans, hung limply on his thin body.

"Lucius", said Harold Ward. "Where am I going to get $200? There are bills to pay and mouths to feed and you want me to give you $200 just so you can go to Palms Springs with your friends? I'm sorry Lucius, but that won't work." Harold had been surprised to see Lucius up so early this morning. Early, that is, for Lucius. Now he realized why. Here it was 8:30 in the morning and Lucius was packed and ready to go out and party.

"Dad", continued Lucius. "It's not like I'm asking for the last money in the world or anything. I just need the money for the weekend. All the guys are going, Dad. I can't just not go."

"If you had kept that job I got you at the garage you would have your own money to go," said Harold. "You should have kept the job." One of Harold's old friends owned the gas station and garage in the center of town. He had needed an extra hand and Harold had suggested Lucius who had a knack for things mechanical. Lucius had originally taken to the job, what with his love for old cars and stuff. He enjoyed tinkering with the engines, tuning them up. Even the oil changes. He would show up for work early and leave late. He was doing great. Then suddenly he quit showing up.

"Yea, right, and missed all the parties because I was working Saturdays. It's not like I'm a charity case or something that I need to work," said Lucius, losing his temper.

"Not a charity case?" Harold was trying hard not to lose his. "If you're not a charity case then why are you standing here begging me for money? Why aren't you out there earning it?"

"You're my Dad. You're supposed to give me money," replied Lucius.

"You're right," Harold sighed. "You're right. I'm supposed to give you money. Well, let's see. I buy your clothes. Put a roof over your head. Feed you. I even paid for that car you're driving." reminded Harold. "But if you think I'm going to give you money so you and your friends can go to Palm Springs and get drunk for the weekend, you're out of your mind."

"So you're not going to give me the money then" asked Lucius.

"No." replied Harold. "I'm not."

"Fine then. I'll go get the money myself. I don't need you," yelled Lucius as he went for the door. "I'll take care of it myself. And don't worry about spending your precious money on me anymore because I'm never..."

Harold couldn't hear the rest as Lucius slammed the door on his way out. What a temper that boy had developed. Harold couldn't figure what had become of him. He was not the same boy anymore. He hadn't quite become a man yet but he wasn't a boy either. He had quit playing base-ball, which he had loved so much. He had been the first baseman on the varsity team in high school. Would have received a scholarship if he hadn't messed around the last half of his senior year. They never went to games together anymore, either. Not since Lucius started hanging out with those weird guys. Listening to that horrible music and wearing those shirts with those dreadful pictures and scenes on them. What was going on with that boy? Where had he gone wrong? Harold wished he could see inside Lucius' head to see what he was thinking. Then Harold wondered where Lucius was going to get the money. He wasn't the same boy and Harold was not sure that Lucius had limits anymore. Harold started thinking that maybe he should just have given Lucius the money. He then put the thoughts aside. It was time for him to get going. He had some errands to run and he had to do them soon or he would be late for work.

CHAPTER THREE

The Cares of This World

"WILL YOU KIDS HURRY UP?" PAMELA YELLED FROM the kitchen. "You're going to miss the bus." Pamela was the manager of the largest bank in town, Greater Metropolitan Federal. She had been promoted just three months ago. She still felt as if she had to make an impression. As if she had to prove she was able to handle the responsibility. She always seemed to be under pressure, always in a hurry. What time was it? Quarter of eight. Plenty of time. No need to rush. "Will you kids hurry?"

Her husband, Tim, came down the stairs chasing Stacey and Tim Jr. ahead of him. "Hurry kids," he said. "Let's don't be late."

"We got lots of time, Dad," said Tim Jr.

"We have lots of time," corrected Stacey. Tim Jr. was the youngest. Always trying to be different. Difficult. Stacey saw it as her job to keep him in line since she was the big sister.

"That's what I said," Tim Jr. responded as he, Stacey and their father sat at the breakfast table. "We got lots of time."

"Mom," Stacey cried out, exasperated. "Can you teach this little creep to speak correctly? He's such a dweeb."

"Mom," Tim Jr. yelled back, mimicking Stacey putting on her makeup. "Can we send Stacey away to the circus? She could be one of the clowns."

"That's enough you two," said Pamela. "Stop teasing each other and eat your breakfast."

"We don't got no breakfast yet," said Tim Jr. sticking his tongue out at his sister.

"Mom," was all Stacey could say.

Pamela put bowls of cold cereal and a carton of milk in front of her husband and children. "Tim," she pleaded.

Tim peered at his children over his morning newspaper giving them his stern look. "Enough," he said. "Timmy. What ever do you plan to be when you grow up with language like that?" Then he looked at Stacey, for the first time that morning really, and noticed that her make up was sort of heavy for a fifteen-year-old.

"Do you think you need that much make up Stacey," he said, dreading a confrontation with his daughter. "You're quite beautiful without it."

Stacey rolled her eyes towards the ceiling then said, "Dad. Everybody wears it like this. Do you want me to be different?"

Tim retreated behind the security of his newspaper and shut out the sounds of the breakfast table, content in the knowledge that he would soon be at work and could forget the burden of raising a family for the rest of the day.

Pamela finally got everybody fed and ready to head out the door. She checked her watch and saw that it was ten after eight. The school bus would pick up the children at 8:15. She would leave home at 8:30. That would put her at work a little before 9:00, in time for the bank opening. She liked to be there for the opening each morning. She really didn't have to be there before ten. Her assistants took care of the opening and teller services. There was nothing for her to do until the actual bank operations started at ten. She just liked to be there. In case she was needed. And she wanted to show her enthusiasm for her new position. It was hard enough for a woman to attain position in the working world and she did not intend to let anything ruin her chance.

She got the kids out the door just in time for the bus, giving each a quick kiss as they went out. Tim followed right behind muttering something about coming home late because of some meeting. Pamela was now alone in the house. She finished her third cup of coffee as she read the financial section of the morning paper. She then re-checked her hair and make up and headed out the door for work, right on time.

CHAPTER FOUR

The Pride Of Your Heart Has Deceived You

"HOW DOES THIS SPOT RIGHT HERE LOOK STU?" asked Kathleen Johnson, the rising star reporter for the local evening news show. "This will give us the academy entrance as a back ground for the opening shot." Kathleen had made a quick rise from the newsroom to a roving reporter in only five years with the station. She was hoping to get an anchor spot in the next few years. She knew she could do it. In fact, her psychic had told her to expect a big change in her position before the end of the month. Wouldn't that be wonderful? Kathleen rubbed the power crystal she kept hanging around her neck on a fine silver chain, feeling the life force flowing from it into her. She would hide the crystal under her blouse just before they took the shot.

"That's great," replied Stuart Cadegan, Kathleen's cameraman. "If we time it just right we might be able to get a shot of one of the academy classes marching past. Maybe even the graduating class." Stu watched Kathleen rub her power crystal and wondered if it really did any good. He figured it must. He knew that there was an unseen power on the earth that helped people. And the way those crystals focused light there was no reason that they shouldn't be able to focus the life forces or what ever it was Kathleen talked about. And Kathleen had sure made a rapid rise. In fact, his career had suddenly zoomed after teaming up with Kathleen a year ago. He made a mental note to ask Kathleen where he could get one of those crystals.

"It's a quarter of nine, Stu," Kathleen interrupted Stu's thoughts. "We better get this intro shot and then go set up for the graduation."

"I'm ready when you are, Kathy," Stu said. "In fact, the junior class is lining up right behind you. What a great shot. O.K. Ready? Three, two, one, roll."

"Good morning. This is Kathleen Johnson, Channel 3 On The Spot News at the Metropolitan Police Academy where today a new batch of police recruits graduate from their intense training period in preparation to take to the streets to protect and serve. What's so unusual about this graduating class? Well, this morning Jacob Crew, the son of Metropolitan Police Chief, Samuel Crew, is graduating and following in his fathers and grandfathers footsteps. Cut." Kathleen made a cutting motion across her neck with her left hand. She would pick up her statement in the next shot showing the actual graduation and Stu would splice it all together editing in footage of Jacob Crew receiving his diploma. They would then broadcast the entire footage on the 10:00 AM news.

"Excellent," said Stu. "We'll use that one. Boy we're good." He smiled at Kathleen and they quickly moved off to prepare for the next shot, happy to have gotten this one in one quick take. Not everybody could do that. He and Kathleen had chemistry though. And power crystals.

CHAPTER FIVE

Who Then is a Faithful And Wise Servant…

JOHN NELSON STOOD INSIDE THE FRONT DOOR OF the Greater Metropolitan Federal Bank, opening the door each time one of the employees arrived and locking it right behind them. He was the security guard at the bank and he took his job seriously. Still, he had a smile and a cheerful good morning for each employee as they came to the door. He knew them all by name. He had been working this same bank for 15 years. Ever since he retired from the Navy, where he had served as a Shore Patrolman. He liked his job. Nothing had ever happened at the bank in those 15 years and he was happy about that.

John saw Pamela Riesling exit the parking lot elevator and start towards the bank's front door. He looked at his watch. Ten minutes till nine. Right on time, he thought.

"Good morning, Mrs. Riesling," John said as he held the door open for her.

"Good morning, John," She responded. "How is everybody this morning?"

"Fine, ma'am," he replied. "Seems everybody is looking forward to this important weekend."

Pamela stopped and looked at John, shock and worry on her face. "What important weekend?" she asked.

"This is the Easter weekend, ma'am," John said.

"Oh," Pamela said, relieved. "Easter egg hunts and all of that." She used to have them for her children but they had out grown those childish games.

"Well," John said. "I mean, today is Good Friday. About 2000 years ago Jesus died for our sins. He arose again in 3 days. That's what this holiday is all about, you know."

John was always eager to tell people about his faith in God. John had come to know the Lord during his time in the Navy, during his second enlistment. He was off duty one Easter Sunday morning, nursing a hangover, when one of his subordinates invited him to the base chapel for church services. John hadn't been to Church since he was a kid and was not really interested in going that morning. But it was Sunday, a holiday and everything in town was closed. He was bored. He decided it would be as interesting to spend an hour in church, as it would be lying in his bunk.

John was never the same. The Chaplain, who had pastored a non-denominational church in California, spoke about things that John had never heard of. He spoke about them so clearly that John was able to understand them. He told John, it seemed as if the Chaplain was speaking directly to John, about Jesus Christ. About His loving sacrifice on the Cross. He explained how Jesus had willingly gone to the cross so that John could be forgiven. He explained how Jesus loved John even before John knew Jesus, while John was still a sinner. And Jesus had still made the sacrifice for him. John was trying to understand that love while the Chaplain continued. Finally he read from Matthew, 4:19 and 20. "'Follow Me and I'll make you fishers of men.' And immediately they dropped the nets and followed," the Chaplain quoted. John thought, "Those men could leave their whole way of life, their livelihood, everything at the call of this Jesus. Now He's calling me. Who am I not to follow?"

John cried in the pew. A Chief Petty Officer in the U.S. Navy, crying in church. His subordinate, who had brought him to church, looked over at his Chief and he knew. He was witnessing a birth. At the end of the service he took John to the front of the church where John spoke to the Chaplain. He told the Chaplain what he was feeling. The Chaplain asked John if he wanted to be a new man, to be part of the family of Jesus Christ. John knew that he did. He was already feeling different. He was feeling free. He wanted that feeling to grow. John accepted Jesus Christ as his Lord and Savior that day. He was never the same after that. From that day on he followed Jesus and looked for men to catch. For the opportunity to tell men about Jesus so they could learn what he had learned.

"Oh, yeah," Pamela laughed. "This is supposed to be a religious holiday, isn't it?" She quickly walked away. She had forgotten that John was one of those holier than thou Christians. Well, he was a good guard. As long as he did his job and didn't bother the customers with that Jesus business she figured it was all right.

John locked the door and watched Pamela walk away. She needs to hear the truth, he thought. Someday I have to corner her and tell her. Someday soon.

CHAPTER SIX

Behold You Are Fair My
Love…

STEPHEN WALSH LOOKED AT HIS WATCH AS HE PARKED
his car in the Greater Metropolitan Federal Bank parking lot. It was almost 9:00. He didn't want to be late. Not a good witness. But his car wouldn't start that morning. By the time he got it started he found he had gotten grease on his shirt. He'd had to run back in and change it. He had been afraid to leave the car running while he went inside but he didn't know if he could get it started again once he turned it off.

Stephen was 25, good looking and had a BA in business from State College. He looked forward to a long career in banking. He had been raised in a Christian home and had attended Christian schools so the stint in State had been somewhat of a culture shock. Still, his beliefs were ingrained and he saw nothing there that made him want to change them. He was not enamored of the party scene and sex remained something he looked forward to whenever he got married. Not that it didn't cross his mind. He was a man after all. He just chose to trust God.

He was now at work so he shut off the ignition and quickly jumped out of his car, locking the door behind him. He started running towards the

16

bank hearing his car sputter and ping behind him as it continued dieseling before finally shutting off. He looked back towards his car just in time to see Kari Pendelton, the new teller, walking rapidly through the cloud of blue-gray smoke left by his car. He saw her wave a delicate hand in front of her face as if that would clear the smoke away so she could breath again.

He had to get a new car, he thought, simultaneously thinking that Kari was absolutely beautiful. Sure wish she knew the Lord, Stephen thought. He slowed to allow her to catch up to him.

"Good morning, Stephen," Kari smiled brightly, if a little breathlessly. "I see you still intend to make your one man stand against the AQMD. At least now I know where air pollution comes from."

"Aw, Kari," Stephen moaned, cut to the quick. "I wish I could afford a new car but I just can't right now. I know that it's a piece of junk but it's the only piece of junk I have."

"It almost didn't start this morning again," he added sheepishly.

"Well, you let me know if you want to start that car pool," Kari said. "You could probably save some money to get a new car, or get that one fixed. And it would be an incentive for me to leave home a little earlier. I hate being late."

"Me, too," said Stephen. "We had better hurry." Stephen thought of being able to ride every morning with Kari. To have her to himself each morning. If only she was Christian, he thought.

Stephen had been assigned to train Kari when she first arrived at the bank. He found that she was a quick learner. She enjoyed her job. And life. She was a very nice girl. Fun to be around. And absolutely beautiful. She stood a short 5'2" but looked taller. She maintained an athletic physique. She played softball and ran track in college and continued to run to keep in shape. Her hair, a not quite blond brown, was cut short and framed her oval face accenting her cat like deep brown eyes. Her nose was slightly upturned. Her lips were full and wide, almost always in a broad toothy smile. The smile showed the one imperfection, a slightly crooked canine, which made the tooth appear pointed. She was the kind of girl Stephen would love to call his own but he was aware that his Christian beliefs could be a problem between them. If not now, then maybe in the future. If only she were a Christian.

They ran the rest of the way to the bank. They saw John unlock the door and hold it open for them.

"Good morning Miss Pendelton, Mr. Walsh. Just in time," said John, looking at his watch then up at the two young tellers.

"Good morning, John," said Kari giving him a large, bashful smile.

"Thank God," said Stephen as he hurried to his teller window. Stephen looked back at John and saw that he hadn't locked the door behind them. He was heading for the back door to unlock it. It was 9:00 AM and the bank was open for business.

∾

CHAPTER SEVEN

Eat, Drink and Be Merry…

At 9:00 AM that Friday morning Charles Watson McGuire sat in the comfortable overstuffed leather chair behind his huge polished oak desk and swiveled towards the huge window behind him, blowing a stream of thick gray smoke from the Craftsman's Bench Maduro #1 hand rolled Honduran cigar. Some of his business associates, others might call them friends, chided him about smoking over the counter Honduran cigars instead of some privately imported expensive Cuban cigar. But McGuire had been smoking his Maduro's for years, since his law practice had first taken off, and he had grown to enjoy them as much as any of the other more expensive cigars. Besides, it always gave him a point of contention that he could argue with the other attorneys on their Wednesday night smoke outs. And being an attorney, he loved a good argument.

McGuire looked out of his 12th floor window taking a deep pull on his cigar. He remembered those long ago lean years, before his firm, Kelter, McGuire and Warner, had taken off. He thought of that one case that started his success. He had almost not taken it, not wanting to devote his time to criminal law. It was a robbery. Some young kid decided that it would be fun to rob the local bank with some friends. They did it as a lark. They went in with guns, three of them, while a fourth, his client, waited in a car. They took over the bank and robbed it. And got caught.

The driver's father called him to defend his son. He was about to turn
the father down when he recognized the man's name. He owned some
large corporation or other and could have used any number of attorneys
but he had called McGuire. McGuire figured that if he could put up a
good defense, file some motions, he could draw the case out and with
appeals it could go on for years. He could milk it for all it was worth. And
with the client's name he was sure to get some press time out of it, which
was sure to mean some more high roller clients in the future. If he didn't
mess the case up. He decided to take the case on.

He met with the defendant and his father and got all of the necessary
information and documents on the case. To his immense joy he found
that some of his client's constitutional rights had been violated and some
evidence had been mishandled. McGuire called several press conferences
and put a lot of information in the news media about police wrongdo-
ing. Eventually, amid all of the hoopla, the charges against his client were
dropped by the district attorney's office. The other three boys were con-
victed of the robbery and received stiff prison sentences.

McGuire was a little disappointed that he was not able to draw the case
out a little longer and that he would not be able to file an appeal, which
reduced his fee considerably. But in the long run it turned out better as the
publicity and the quick success got him much more attention, which, as it
turned out, brought him many more high profile clients. Some of which
were still with him.

McGuire was then able to form a partnership with Tom Kelter and
Andy Warner, both excellent attorneys. They had then developed the firm
into a multi-million-dollar law firm with several junior attorneys and many
other employees.

Today, though, McGuire had other plans. He was going to make a
small, but possibly lucrative, investment that his partners did not know
about. He would have to use some of the firm's money to make the investment but he would be able to pay it all back as soon as the investment
began to pay off. He couldn't borrow the money from the firm because
his partners might think the investment was not totally above board,
which it might not be. But as long as he didn't know for sure that something illegal was happening he felt the investment was worth the risk. He
had an appointment at the firm's bank, Greater Metropolitan Federal, at

10:00 AM today to close the deal. The bank manager didn't realize that he was borrowing the firm's money under questionable circumstances and barring any unforeseen developments there should be no reason for anyone to find out.

CHAPTER EIGHT

୭ଚ

Go to the Ant
You Sluggard…

AT 9:00 AM RICHARD COPAS CALLED HIS SON, Fredo, to remind him that Richard needed a ride to the bank that morning. He had asked Fredo to pick him up at nine so he could get to the bank early. Richard looked out of the window again, hoping against hope that maybe, just maybe, this time Fredo would show up on time. As usual, his son was late. Richard was 65 but looked older. He had been a gardener since his teens. He had been able to buy his own equipment and start his own business early on, but gardening was a tough job. The years had taken their toll and he had been forced to retire. The pain in his back and hands just didn't allow him to work any more. Richard's wife had died just a year ago after 47 years of marriage. He still missed her. His children were all grown. Some had married and moved away. They had all gone to college and now had good, respectable jobs. Except Fredo. Fredo was the youngest and somehow he just couldn't make good.

Richard picked up the phone angrily and dialed Fredo's number, wondering if Fredo was even home. He could never be sure if Fredo made it home the previous night. He was not even sure what Fredo did everyday especially so late at night. But Fredo usually had enough money so it must be a pretty good job. Or something.

"Hello," Fredo sleepily answered the phone.

"I thought you were going to pick me up this morning to take me to the bank," Richard said forgoing the niceties of a greeting.

"Oh, Pop. I forgot. I'll be there right away," Fredo said and hung up. Fredo thought he would have to drop his Pop off at the bank and let him take the bus home. He had to meet with some of the guys at ten. If only he had gotten to bed earlier. But then Beto had shown up with that extra six-pack. Oh, well. Nothing he could do about it now.

Fredo was 23. He had dropped out of high school. He had later tested for and received his GED. Still, jobs were few and far between for someone with no skills. Good jobs at least. Yet he was always able to manage some odd jobs. Enough to pay for the single room he rented. And food. And of course the beer. The day was not complete without at least a six-pack.

He dragged himself out of bed and put on the same jeans and T-shirt he had been wearing last night. His room had a small shower but he had to pay his share of the water bill. And he was in a hurry this morning.

CHAPTER NINE

For God Has Not Given Us A Spirit Of Fear

MARY BROWN LOOKED AT HER WATCH AND SAW THAT it was 9:00 AM. The bus should be here in just a couple of minutes. She really hated taking the bus, but since her car had broken down she had to ride it if she intended to go anywhere. Her husband, Roger, needed his car to get to work and they couldn't afford to buy another one. Meanwhile she had to get to the bank to pay the mortgage on their house. It was already over due and if she didn't pay it today there would be late charges and she couldn't afford those. Especially since Roger would get mad. Mary didn't like making Roger mad.

Mary had married Roger right out of high school. She had been in love then. Roger seemed like a very special man. Everyone in the school loved Roger. They should. He was the track, football and basketball star. He had been offered a college scholarship and was going to play pro ball one day. Mary was popular in school also. She and Roger soon started dating. They became an item. Mary became pregnant by the future star half way through her senior year. They would get married right after graduation. Her future was secure.

Then came the injury, a busted knee during the Homecoming Game. Roger would never play sports again. There would be no college scholarship. Not only did that deprive Roger of any chance of playing pro ball, he could not afford to go to college without the scholarship. There would be no high paying job following a lucrative sports career.

Roger became angry at life and took it out on Mary. Now 40 and married 22 years, Mary had three adult children who were still living at home. Mary had become frightened of Roger. She had also become frightened of just about everything else. Crime ran rampant. Kids were selling drugs on the street corners. Siren's wailing all night long. She was a prisoner in her own home.

Mary saw the bus approaching and got up from the bus bench, getting nearer to the bus stop sign. She wanted to make sure the bus driver saw her. It would be thirty minutes before the next bus arrived. She already had the 45-minute ride into town to deal with. Probably a half-hour in the bank. Another 45 minutes to get home and that was two hours out of her day. She had so many other things to do today. Before Roger came home.

Mary waited until the doorway was clear of alighting passengers and wearily climbed the stairs onto the bus. She counted out the bus fare, exact change, and deposited it in the fare box then looked for an empty seat that was semi clean and moved in to it, helped by the sudden motion of the bus starting forward. She stared out the window trying to avoid the looks of the other passengers. She did not want to encourage any conversation. You never knew who rode the busses these days. "Oh, I hate these busses," she thought, then resumed her vigil looking for Center Street where she would get off and walk the one block to the Greater Metropolitan Federal Bank, which held the note on her home.

CHAPTER TEN

❦

…The Sword of the Spirit…

AT 9:00 AM SAMUEL CRUE WAS SEATED IN THE FRONT row of seats at the academy auditorium. Stephanie was seated next to him, on his right. Next to Stephanie was Captain Vanderhoof with his wife seated next to him followed by other department and academy brass with their wives or guests. Samuel looked at Vanderhoof and thought he was rather pompous looking. Arthur Lawrence Vanderhoof III. A short, tense, schooled man with bright red hair, he was proud of his rank at the department and always made sure that everyone knew exactly who he was. As a matter of fact, his wife introduced him as Captain Vanderhoof of the Police Department at social events. And she was Mrs. Captain Vanderhoof. Samuel didn't particularly like Vanderhoof, who headed up the department's patrol division, but he had to deal with it. Vanderhoof had made captain and that was that. Samuel said a quick prayer for forgiveness for his thoughts of Vanderhoof and for continued strength in dealing with him.

Vanderhoof looked over at Samuel. Samuel leaned across Stephanie towards Vanderhoof and said, "It's 9:00 AM. Lets get this show on the road."

"Yes, Chief," Vanderhoof responded nodding. Vanderhoof didn't quite like Samuel, either. He thought Samuel was too lax. Too easy on the men.

He didn't like the fact that the other captains, and even the lieutenants, called him Samuel. He was the Chief for Pete's sake. Where was their respect? He had watched all of the military movies. Battan, The Big Red One. He saw how superior officers were addressed. By their rank! As should be. And it should be that way here. Vanderhoof had never served in the military.

Vanderhoof hoped to be Chief himself one day. Maybe when Samuel retired, which he hoped would be soon. He would then put these slackers in their place. He would institute stiff discipline and proper protocol. Everyone would be addressed by his or her proper rank. One day.

Vanderhoof looked towards the end of the auditorium stage and caught the attention of one of the academy staff, giving him the signal to start the ceremony. He then looked at his wife to be sure she had seen him give the command that everyone had been waiting for. She gave Vanderhoof a smug smile. Vanderhoof's narrow chest expanded a good inch.

Suddenly from the right side of the stage a young man in a brand new police uniform appeared. His haircut was fresh, his face newly shaven, his skin was tan. He looked lean and hard from the months of physical activity at the academy. His back ramrod straight, eyes focused straight ahead, he marched into the auditorium and directly to the first row of seats behind the Chief, followed by about 60 other brand new officers. They all marched directly to their seats and stood before them at the position of attention. At a command from one of the academy staff all of the new officers sat as one.

Captain Vanderhoof then walked onto the stage and marched to a point behind the podium, looking somewhat comical in his exaggerated attempt to impart a commanding presence. For some reason Samuel thought of a Keystone Cop. Vanderhoof, who would emcee the affair, welcomed the guests to the graduation and started the ceremony.

The first order of business was the benediction. Vanderhoof had insisted that there be no benediction. "Not in this day and age," he insisted. But Samuel would have none of that. God first in everything. And God was God. In the beginning, He was now and He would be forevermore. Regardless of the era, there would be a benediction.

The department Chaplain, Peter McGee, a reserve officer with the department who was also the Pastor at a local church, handled the benediction.

Peter McGee approached the podium. "Let's call on the Lord," he said simply. Peter bowed his head and closed his eyes.

"Dear Lord, our blessed Heavenly Father," he prayed. "We gather here today, in Your presence, the friends and family of a group of young men and women who have decided to devote their lives in Your service, Father."

Vanderhoof looked sharply at Peter. What did he mean by "Your service"? They were entering into the city's service, not the ministry.

"We ask You dear Father," Peter continued unaware of Vanderhoof's objections, "to keep Your hand on these young men and women. That You lead them and guide them. That You help them to understand that in becoming police officers they are, in fact, entering into Your service. For in Romans 13 You tell us that all authorities are appointed by God, that those authorities are Your ministers to man for good. But also that those authorities do not bear the sword in vain."

Vanderhoof did not like where this was leading. Who said God appointed the authorities? He had been appointed by the Mayor himself.

"We also ask, precious Father," Peter continued, "that You protect and encourage the families of these young officers. That You help them to adjust to the fears, frustrations and new lifestyles that come with being a police officer, or the family member of one of those officers. We further pray Dear Lord that You protect police officers the world over. Keep them safe, physically and spiritually, as You help them to keep us safe. We pray these things in Jesus precious and holy name. Amen."

Peter smiled at the assembly and walked off of the stage. Vanderhoof resumed his position behind the podium. He had intended to give a searing lecture designed to start the new officers in the proper direction of respect for rank and the chain of command but Peter's comments had so infuriated him that he lost all composure. He chose instead to proceed directly to the pledge of allegiance. This was something he was a little more comfortable with. He asked everyone to rise then led the pledge himself, facing the flag, placing his hand over his heart and reciting the well-known words, realizing too late that he also would have to acknowledge God.

Vanderhoof turned back to the podium and said solemnly, "Esteemed colleagues, fellow officers, ladies and gentlemen, may I present the Chief of Police of the Metropolitan Police Department, Chief Samuel Crue."

Samuel rose from his chair, embarrassed by the applause, and walked onto the stage. As he did so Kathleen urged Stuart to get a shot of the Chief walking across the stage and taking the podium. Kathleen felt they could use that as the next shot on the video with a voice over from her. The shot would then fade to the Chief's son receiving his diploma, which would fade back to Kathleen as she completed her story. Stuart agreed with Kathleen. He started the camera rolling and kept it focused on the Chief.

This was great, Stuart thought. None of the other news agencies were here. This was pretty big news and he was going to have the only video available. This was turning out to be a good day. He was sure happy to be working with Kathleen.

Samuel shook hands with Vanderhoof then turned to the microphone, allowing time for Vanderhoof to leave the stage.

"Good morning Ladies and Gentlemen, fellow officers, Graduating Class" Samuel began. "Welcome to what amounts to both an end and a beginning. Today the members of the graduating class end their time in the academy, and their old life. With the commitment that they began four months ago, and confirm today, they begin a new life. A life dedicated to the service of others. Family, friends, loved ones, you embark on that journey with them. After today your life will also be changed. Every hour that these young men and women spend in a patrol car, your heart will be there with them. When they are up all night working the graveyard shift, it is you who have to give them up. When they work on the weekends and holidays, it is you who will have to do without them. Every time these people give, when they put themselves in danger to help others, it is you who give. Today you are giving these young men and women to your neighbors, to your communities. You are giving away a dear part of your life so that others may walk the streets in safety."

"Graduating Class," he continued. "You who are dedicating your lives to ensure the safety of others, what does it mean to be a police officer?"

Samuel scanned the new officers' faces. "I was going to talk to you about one chapter, the thirteenth chapter, of the book of Romans from the Bible but Chaplain McGee has already made clear that you are in a position that is appointed by God. You are in His service, whether you understand that or not."

"What does God have to do with being a police officer, you may ask yourself," Samuel said pointedly. "Our founding fathers made America a country whose basic laws were founded in Christian doctrine. George Washington said that to remove God from government would begin the decline of that government. Our laws are based on the Judeo-Christian ethics taught in the Ten Commandments. In our earliest schools children were taught to read by reading the Bible and the Ten Commandments. Today those have been removed from our schools. Look at what is happening to our government. Look at our youth running rampant in the streets without direction, resorting to drugs for compassion, sex for love, gangs for family. Today's generation is amoral. Our nation has turned away from God. We have removed God from our government, our schools, and our families. We have allowed great evils to infect our land in the name of progress. And these are the evils that you are going out to face. The evils you are going to protect your community from. Your heart will have to be in the right place to accomplish that task without falling into evil yourself."

Looking down at the young, fresh faces looking back up at him he continued, "In these past four months we have strived to give you a knowledge of the laws, skills and tactics that you will need to succeed as a police officer. I want to leave you with two more things. Temper everything else you have learned through these."

"First, let me quote from Second Chronicles, chapter seven, verse fourteen. God is talking to King Samuel about the evil in the land because the people have turned away from God," Samuel explained. "He says, 'If My people, who are called by My name, shall humble themselves, and pray, and seek My face, and turn from their wicked ways, then I will hear from heaven and will forgive their sin and will heal their land.'"

"Second, from the 23rd Psalm, verse 4," he quoted, "'Yea though I walk through the valley of the shadow of death, I will fear no evil for You are with me.'"

"Remember these things," Samuel cautioned. "Remember what Chaplain McGee said. Remember that you are the servant. The badge does not give you any authority to bully or have people bow to your will. It gives you the authority to serve. Do not fear to serve. Serve well, in humility, using your badge as a shield against evil, for yourself as well as for others. Keep your eyes open, your wit's about you and God in your heart. And go home to your families safely each night."

"God bless you all," Samuel said. "And I'll see you on the streets."

CHAPTER ELEVEN

❦

They Enter at the Windows Like a Thief

WHILE SAMUEL WALKED UP TO THE PODIUM TO BEGIN his speech, Lucius walked around to the back of his friend Ted's house. Lucius and Ted had known each other since first grade. Lucius was always welcome at Ted's house. Ted had even shown Lucius where the extra key was kept in the planter by the back door in case one of the family lost their key. Lucius knew no one would be home right now. Ted was at work, since there was no school today. His parents would be at work, too.

Lucius went to the planter and found the key, right where it was supposed to be. He used it to let himself in Ted's back door. He knew what he was doing was wrong but it wasn't his fault. It was his dad's fault. Lucius would show him. "Don't give me money," Lucius thought. "I told him I could get it myself. And I will. He'll see."

Lucius went into the house and found his way to the basement door. Lucius knew that Ted's father kept his safe down there. Lucius remembered several years ago when he and Ted had been playing in the basement. They had almost been caught down there. Ted had been forbidden to go into the basement. That just made it all the more mysterious. He and Ted could not resist the temptation to explore the basement. There were so many neat things down there. So many dark spaces that they could crawl into and explore. And hide.

Lucius remembered. He had been so scared when Ted's father came into the basement. They had both been standing in front of the safe, wondering what was in it. What kind of treasures did Ted's dad have that he needed so large a safe to hide it all? All those years ago the safe seemed enormous to a small boy. Upon hearing Ted's dad coming, they realized that they needed to hide. They ran to one of the crawl spaces under the house and quickly jumped into it. They crawled into the darkness. Lucius turned, panting, afraid. He watched Ted's dad enter the basement. His excitement was heightened when he saw Ted's dad go to the safe. He turned the combination dial on the door, first this way then that, and then pulled the handle. Nothing happened. Ted's dad tried the dial again and pulled the handle again. Again nothing happened. Lucius was disappoint-ed. He thought he was going to see Ted's dad's treasure. But the door wouldn't open.

Lucius watched as Ted's dad went over to his workbench, an old desk really, and removed a ring of keys from a nail on the wall over the desk. He used one of the keys to open the top desk drawer. Ted's dad pulled out an old, yellowed, folded sheet of notebook paper. He unfolded it as he went back to the safe. Ted's dad then started turning the dial as he read from the sheet of paper. It was the combination. He turned the dial and pulled the handle. The click was so loud that Lucius almost screamed. Ted's dad folded the sheet of paper and put it back in the desk drawer, locked it, then hung the keys back in their place.

Ted's dad then returned to the safe and started opening the door. Lucius watched in rapt anticipation, imagining stories of pirates and bur-ied treasures. As the door came open Lucius saw something he had only seen on television before. He had heard about them. Had even played with toy ones. But never in his wildest imagination had he ever seen any-thing like this. The safe was full of guns. There were rifles, shotguns and pistols. Some were small. Some were big. Some were very big. All were scary looking and beautiful in the way they reflected the light off of their dark metal skins. Lucius watched as Ted's dad removed one of the rifles, took it to the desk and expertly took it apart and lovingly cleaned it.

It was about an hour later that Ted's dad had finished his work and put the rifle away. In the boredom of waiting the novelty and beauty of the guns wore away. Lucius just wished Ted's dad would hurry and leave so he and Ted could go play. While he was waiting he took the time to look at each of the guns in the safe. From this distance he could just make the outline of most of them. Then he saw it, right in the center of the safe. It was a dark, deadly treasure sitting there so menacing, so inviting. Who ever had that treasure could own the world. Then Ted's dad finished. He put the rifle back and locked the safe, pulling the handle hard to ensure that it was locked, and then left the basement. Lucius never got to see those guns again but he remembered where they were.

Now here he was in the basement again standing in front of the safe. It didn't seem so big anymore. He wondered if it still contained its deadly treasure. Lucius went to the desk and removed the key ring from its nail. He tried several keys before he found the one that opened the desk. There was the yellowed sheet of paper, still folded. He carefully unfolded it and read the combination. He went to the safe and spun the dial, matching the numbers on the paper, right 75, left 2, right 24. Lucius pulled the handle. The click scared him again. Just like so many years ago. Lucius folded the paper and put it back in the desk, locking it and replacing the keys.

Lucius returned to the safe and began opening the door, anxious to see the treasure hidden inside but wanting to savor the moment. Ever since he had decided on what to do, when he had remembered about Ted's father's safe after all of these years, he had been so excited. He was going to make the trip to Palm Springs. He was going to book a large expensive room for himself, and his friends. Heck, he would book a room for each of them. They would eat in style. Drink all they wanted. They would be able to entertain all of the girls. He couldn't wait. He was going to have plenty of money. He was going to party in style. As soon as he got the treasure out of the safe.

Lucius looked into the safe and there it was, in the same place. Right in the center was a clean, shiny, well-oiled Thompson sub-machine gun. Lucius reached into the safe and removed the Thompson. It felt good in his hands. It was heavier than he had imagined, and cold. He had never held a real gun in his hands. Now he was holding the king of all guns, he thought. He had seen those World War Two movies where the hero always had one. And the 1920's gangster movies always had tons of them.

Lucius found a stick magazine loaded with 30 rounds of .45 caliber ammunition. After a few minutes of studying the Thompson, he figured out how to insert the magazine. He then worked the bolt and loaded the gun. He looked into the safe, ready to close it when he saw a brace of .45 caliber semi-automatic pistols. He put the Thompson down and picked up the pistols. He slid them into his waistband, one behind each hip. They felt good. Better to have too much firepower, he thought, than not enough. He suddenly fancied himself Melvin Purvis then decided he was more like John Dillinger. What made him think of those names, he wondered? Lucius looked at his watch and saw that it was 9:20 AM. Time for him to go.

CHAPTER TWELVE

✎

This is My Beloved Son…

SAMUEL HAD FINISHED HIS SPEECH. VANDERHOOF walked to the podium but stood to the side until the applause died down. What are they all clapping about, wondered Vanderhoof? It was just another of the Chief's wishy-washy speeches about returning to God. Vanderhoof knew that the only thing that was going to get the world back on track was to stop crime. And the only way to stop crime was for men, real men like him, to put a stop to it, once and for all. None of this mystical God business. Just a group of good hard men bent on taking it to the crooks and getting rid of them, one way or another. But Vanderhoof knew how to play the game. His turn would come. He applauded and smiled with everybody else.

When the applause died down Vanderhoof briefly took his place behind the podium and continued the game, turning it to his profit. "Ladies and gentlemen," he said. "Chief Vanderhoof." He started the applause once again, seeking to identify himself with Samuel's speech and thus his success.

When the applause died down again Vanderhoof took the podium once more. "Each year the academy graduates four classes," he said. "They each receive the same training. They have the same instructors. Yet each class is different. Each class brings its individual image to the academy guided by the talents of the individual cadets in the class.

"This class is no different," he continued. "Therefore, in each class we try to identify the one cadet who has been the rallying point for his, or her, peers. The one cadet who seems to push his classmates that one step further. That one cadet who gives his all and then some to the career he is pursuing. We call that cadet the Honor Cadet."

"The choice is never easy", Vanderhoof said, enjoying his spot in the limelight. "Some cadets excel in the academics. Others in physical fitness. And still others in the myriad other skills they must learn to be police officers. Still, a choice must be made. The choice for this class is fitting. This cadet was the top cadet academically and was in the top five percent in physical fitness, arrest control and firearms training."

"Ladies and gentlemen," said Vanderhoof. "May I present the Honor Cadet for this class, Cadet Jacob Crue."

CHAPTER THIRTEEN

❦

I Do Not Know the Man

FREDO FINALLY ARRIVED AT RICHARDS'S HOUSE. Richard was waiting outside for him so Fredo didn't have to bother getting out of the car. Fredo shouted, "Come on Pop. Let's go or we'll be late."

"We're already late, mijo." Richard said. "I wanted to be there when the bank opened. You know how I hate the long lines. And they'll be especially crowded today, I think."

"Why would they be crowded today?" asked Fredo.

"Que tonto!" chastened Richard. "Today is Good Friday. Or don't you remember those things anymore. Everybody is going to be running around buying Easter clothes and getting ready to go to grandma's."

"Oh, yeah!" Fredo remembered. "This is the week when all the good looking girls go to Palm Springs."

"Yeah, Palm Springs." Richard said sarcastically. "Now let's go. It's already 9:30."

CHAPTER FOURTEEN

⁓

Seeing the Multitudes, He Went up on a Mountain

JACOB CRUE MOUNTED THE STEPS TO THE STAGE AND walked, marched actually, to the podium. Once at the podium he acknowledged and thanked Vanderhoof, accepting the handshake of his new superior.

"Thank you, Captain Vanderhoof," Jacob started. "Ladies and gentlemen, family and friends, fellow officers, Chief Crue," he continued. "Today we have finally reached a day many of us thought would never arrive. For some of us, it didn't. We started four months ago with a class of 120 cadets. For various reasons 50 of us are not here today. Those of us that remain have endured the rigors of the academy, physical and academic, in order to start our chosen careers, serving the people of our community. You."

Jacob paused shortly trying to accustom himself to this public speaking. "Today ends our academy training," he added, "but it does not end our learning. This is just the beginning. The beginning of our service. Our ministry. Those here today in the blue uniform have all been called into a unique service. A service in which we willingly face certain dangers to ensure that you are safe."

"Are you getting this," Kathleen said. "Make sure you get it all. This kid is pretty good."

"Yeah," said Stuart. "I started with the captain's intro. We can cut that out and edit this kid's speech. Splice in some of the Chiefs speech with your intro and voice-overs. It'll be great."

"Good, Stu," Kathleen encouraged. "Just make sure you get good clean footage. I can't believe we're the only one's here. And listen to this God nonsense they're talking about. This kid is just like his father. Could he be the next chief? What a story!"

CHAPTER FIFTEEN

For Nothing is Secret
That Will Not Be Revealed

IT WAS 9:40 AM. TIME FOR MCGUIRE TO LEAVE HIS office for the bank. McGuire called his secretary. "Janet," he said. "I'll be out of the office for a while. I'm going to buy the missus a gift. I'll be back within the hour."

"Yes Mr. McGuire," said Janet, surprised. He usually sent her out to buy gifts for Mrs. McGuire. It wasn't even her birthday or their anniversary. The old coot is finally getting it, she thought. "Have a good time, sir," she added.

McGuire put on his coat, grabbed his hat and put his cigar in his mouth. He then walked out of his office, taking the elevator to the first floor instead of to the parking garage. He doffed his hat as he exited the elevator, tipping it at the surprised security guards. He then left the building and turned left onto Center Street. It would be an easy 10-minute walk to the bank. He even had time to stop at Arturo's, his favorite cigar shop, to stock up. He still had a few of the Number 1's left but there was no sense in letting the supply get too low.

Jacob was just completing his speech as McGuire turned onto Center Street. "Today, Ladies and Gentlemen, we enter into this service, dedicating ourselves to making our community safe for those that we love," Jacob said. "We hope and pray that we measure up to the task. We will give our all to doing just that. Thank you very much."

Vanderhoof returned to the podium as Jacob marched back to his seat. He waited for the applause to die down then said, "Thank you, Officer Crue."

Without any further ado," he added, trying to avoid focusing any more attention to this God business, "let's graduate the class." He nodded at the Senior Class Counselor.

Chief Vanderhoof returned to the podium as the Senior Class Counselor shouted a series of commands at the graduating class. The class stood smartly to attention, then turned to face right in response to the appropriate commands. Then, row by row, they marched to the podium where they received their graduation certificates from the Chief.

"O.K., Stu," said Kathleen, almost breathlessly. "This is it. I can't believe we're getting all of this and no one else showed up."

Kathleen was elated. She would have the only piece on the academy graduation. With the Chief's son being picked as the honor cadet. Oh, she could have fun with that. And all of this God business. Is that what the people want their police to be like. Right wing God crazies? Oh, she was going to have fun with this.

"Yeah," Stu said, feeling Kathleen's excitement. "I thought for sure that Channel 12 would be here. They're the pro-cop folks aren't they?" Stu liked it when Kathleen got excited. She flushed a little and the way she started talking and moving around. She looked so beautiful when she was excited. Stu was happy to be working with Kathleen again today.

"I'll be sure to get footage of the Chief giving his son the diploma," Stu said. "Maybe I should zoom in on the exchange. Maybe we'll get some good eye contact between them or catch the Chief saying something to his son." He was trying to encourage Kathleen, to keep the excitement going. She sure is something special, he thought.

"That's a good idea, Stu," Kathleen offered. "Get me something good. Then we'll go back to the station and edit this. We should be ready for the 4:00 news. Channel 12 won't be happy. Not happy at all. I think I'm going to buy you a beer when we're done."

"You're on," Stu said. He could barely control himself. She was asking him out. Maybe he could turn a beer into dinner or something.

Kathleen looked at her watch. It was 5 minutes to 10:00. Plenty of time and nobody else was here!

❧

CHAPTER SIXTEEN

The Devil Walks About Like a Roaring Lion

STEPHEN SAT AT HIS TELLER WINDOW RECOUNTING his available cash for the fifth time. He was trying to appear busy but was running out of things to do. Since the bank opened at 9:00 AM not a single customer had come in. He looked at his watch. It was 5 minutes until 10:00. He figured he would take the opportunity to take a short break. Who knows what the rest of the day would be like?

"I'm going to the restroom," he whispered to Kari as he locked his drawer. "I'll be right back."

"Well, hurry up," Kari quipped. "Don't leave me here alone with all of these customers." She offered her lovely smile.

She is so beautiful, Stephen thought. He thought about her previous marriage and how the clod had left her after their child was born. Kari said she had never heard from the guy again after their divorce. Whoever that was that dumped her and left her with the kid was not all there. Not all there at all.

Kari watched Stephen leave and thought of what a really nice person he was. She thought that he was the kind of guy who would make a great husband and father. She wondered what had drawn her to that selfish clod she had been married to. What had she seen in him? What had she been thinking? Well, now she had a child to raise and no guy like Stephen would be interested in a relationship with a ready made family. Still, Stephen was the nicest guy. She wondered if his religious beliefs had any thing to do with that. She was sure it did.

Fredo pulled into the bank parking lot and stopped in the roadway waiting for Richard to get out.

"You going to come in with me, mijo," Richard asked.

"No, Pop," answered Fredo a little self-consciously. "I got to go meet with some guys right now. It might lead to a job."

"What kind of Job," Richard wanted to know.

"I don't know, Pop," Fredo answered hastily. "They just said they had some work lined up. I got to get there. Can you take the bus home?"

"I don't have much choice, do I?" Richard answered testily.

"I'll come by and see you later, Pop," Fredo said solicitously.

Richard got out of Fredo's car and walked towards the bank doors. He wondered what Fredo was up to this time. He knew Fredo was going to wind up in jail again. Fredo wouldn't learn. Richard reached the bank doors just as Stephen entered the employee lounge.

John opened the door for Richard and said, "Good morning, Sir."

"Good morning," answered Richard. "It's not crowded," he added. "I thought it would be crowded."

"You're our first customer this morning," John explained. "Business should start picking up any minute now."

Just a couple of minute's earlier Mary Brown's bus had arrived at Center Street. Warily, Mary got off of the bus through the front door, thanking the driver as she reached the pavement. She looked around her as if to get her bearings. Actually she was looking for danger. Too many crooks on the streets today. Satisfied that she could reach the bank safely, Mary started down Center St. intent on the bank. She avoided making eye contact on the street. No sense in giving anyone an opportunity to start a conversation with her. The fewer people she had contact with the fewer people who could hurt her.

Mary walked rapidly and reached the bank in just a few minutes. She saw the banks guard holding the door open for some Mexican man. The man was older so he was probably no threat. It was those young ones, Mary thought. Hoods, all of them. If she could just make it to the bank safely she would be all right.

Finally, after what seemed like an hour, Mary reached the bank. John held the door open and said, "Good morning."

"Good morning", Mary answered, grateful for the presence of the guard, still not wanting to make conversation. She walked straight for the teller line. There was only one teller operating, a woman, and the Mexican had got to her first. Well, Mary thought, it shouldn't take too long. Then she could head for the safety of her own home.

Just as Mary was getting off of the bus Lucius Ward was parking his car in the bank parking lot. He had made sure to park his car where it was not clearly visible from the bank yet not too far away. He wanted to get to it quickly but he didn't want anybody to get the license number. This was so easy Lucius thought. Why didn't everybody rob banks? There was nothing to this. Lucius got out of the car, leaving the door unlocked. He didn't want to have to fumble with the lock when he was ready to leave. He wondered for a second if someone would steal his car. He laughed out loud as he realized that he was the one doing the stealing today. No one was going to steal his car.

As Lucius was laughing, McGuire was walking towards the bank doors. McGuire saw a Black female, Mary Brown, enter the bank. He hoped it wouldn't be crowded. But he was glad it wouldn't be empty. He didn't want to be the center of attention. His reason for being at the bank was not entirely legal after all. He didn't want anyone asking questions. Or anyone remembering his being there. He would just deal with the bank manager, get his business done and be gone with no one the wiser.

McGuire reached the bank door, which was held open by John. "Good morning, sir." John said.

"Good morning," McGuire answered gruffly, slightly taken aback by John's professional, yet friendly, manner. McGuire walked past John into the bank looking for the bank manager's office. John's firm had banked here for years and this was the first time John had actually been in the bank. He was surprised to see only desks along one wall with bank employees behind some of them, studiously at work. He tried to discern which would be the manager's desk. He then noticed a glass walled cubicle in one corner of the room. A very professional looking middle-aged woman was seated behind the sole desk in the cubicle. That had to be the manager McGuire thought as he started for the cubicle. He stopped himself, not wanting to approach the wrong person. He'd ask. He turned back towards the door where the security guard had been.

John just then opened the door for a strange looking young man. The young man was wearing an old, large overcoat, although the weather was not in the least bit cold. As the young man entered the bank John greeted him with his usual "Good morning'. The young man stopped just inside the door and turned to John. He seemed about to say something. John sensed that something was not right, yet 15 years at the same position had taught him that nothing was going to happen at this bank. Nothing ever happened at the bank.

"Excuse me." John turned to see that McGuire had returned to him. "Where is the bank manager? I have an appointment."

John turned from the young man and was just about to take McGuire to Pamela's desk when he saw a strange look come over McGuire's face. It was a look of shock and horror. McGuire took a couple of steps back from John.

"No. Excuse me." John heard the young man behind him say. John turned to see Lucius Ward standing just inside the bank door with a Thompson M1 sub-machine gun in his right hand and an old Colt M1911 semi-auto pistol in his left. John recognized both arms. Both were .45 caliber guns and both appeared to be in excellent condition.

CHAPTER SEVENTEEN

❧

We Will Rejoice and Be Glad in It

BACK AT THE ACADEMY, STEPHANIE LOOKED ON proudly as Samuel had just finished giving the graduating class their certificates. The class was lined up, in platoon formation, in the orchestra. As each Cadet had received his or her certificate they had marched smartly off the stage and took up their position, standing at parade rest, in their respective squad. When the last person in the squad was in position the squad leader gave the command, Attention! The entire squad moved as one. The class stood with their backs to the audience, their eyes focused on some imaginary spot beyond the stage before them. Their heels locked together, feet at a forty-five degree angle. The arms hanging at their sides, the thumb along the seam of the trousers. The silence in the room could be felt, almost as a presence, interrupted only by a muffled cough, someone shuffling their feet impatiently. Somewhere in the auditorium a baby cried.

Samuel looked at the class giving them a last cursory inspection. They all wore their Class "A" Uniform. Long sleeve blue wool shirts with blue tie and gold clasp, blue wool trousers, blue barracks cap with gold shield and black hatband. They each wore a gold whistle chain, one end clipped to the right epaulet and the other end in the right pocket, a remembrance to years gone by when officers actually carried whistles as a means of communication. And white gloves, which most would never wear again as they were used only for ceremony or parade. And each had a shiny gold badge pinned proudly on their left breast. Samuel approved. The instructors had done an exceptional job with this class. Only one thing left to do.

"Cadet's, au-ten, hu," Samuel growled from the pit of his stomach, sounding every bit the Marine Drill Instructor as he called the class to attention. This was the last time these young men and women would be called cadets. They had made it. And they knew it. Samuel paused as he felt the tension rise, almost expecting the class to explode if he waited too long.

"Raise your right hands," he commanded, then he swore them in. Right hands raised, in unison, they repeated the Police Officers Oath.

"Police officers," he resumed, raising a gasp from the audience. "At the prescribed time and location," the Tac Instructors had advised each cadet what his assignment and reporting time would be, "report to your respective Watch Commander's for assignment. Dismissed!"

Instantly there was an explosion of sound in the auditorium as each brand new police officer let out a cheer. Most threw their hats into the air. Many hugged their classmates. Some gave high fives. Several actually broke into tears of joy.

Those in the audience looked on unsurely, glancing at Samuel then at the crowd of blue, hoping to see their loved one. They wanted to join the celebration but didn't know if they should. Samuel, seeing their distress, nodded at the crowd and waved them forward. Immediately the crowd surged slowly forward, each person seeking out their son or daughter, their brother or sister, their police officer. The young police officers started breaking away from each other and started looking for family and friends. The hugs, high fives and crying started anew.

Samuel scanned the crowd. Over on one end he saw Jacob and Stephanie meet and hug. He could tell by the look on Stephanie's face that she was crying. As she and Jacob held each other Stephanie looked up at Samuel. Samuel smiled at her, gave one last look over the crowd gathered before him, then left the stage satisfied that he had done all that he could do to prepare these young men and women for the task ahead of them. If only they remembered that it was a task of love.

Samuel joined Jacob and Stephanie at the back of the auditorium where he and Jacob embraced.

"Congratulations, son," Samuel said, stepping back from Jacob yet keeping both hands on his son's shoulders. Samuel looked Jacob up and down.

Nodding his head he looked over at Stephanie. "You've done well, Mrs. Crue," he said.

"I had some good help," Stephanie said, sliding under Samuel's left arm and putting her right around his waist. "And good material to work with," she added as Jacob allowed Samuel to put his right arm around his shoulders.

The three of them walked around the auditorium for a while greeting the other new officers and meeting their families. Stephanie had always been proud of Samuel, especially since he had been named Chief. She had enjoyed playing the role of Chief's wife. Now she had the pleasant burden of being the young cop's mother and she was enjoying that role already.

Vanderhoof met Samuel in the midst of the crowd where he had been going along congratulating the young officers and offering his sage advice. He congratulated the three of them.

"I'll be looking forward to you working for me," Vanderhoof told Jacob. "It will be a pleasure having the bosses son under my command. You should be able to do an excellent job for us considering your success in the academy."

"I'll do my best to live up to the expectations," Jacob said, accepting Vanderhoof's handshake.

"I'm going to get back to the station Chief. Make sure everything's going fine," Vanderhoof said.

"Yea. I'll be there soon myself," Samuel answered. "As soon as I can break away from here."

"Yes, Sir," Vanderhoof said. "Ma'am," he added, tipping his hat to Stephanie. Vanderhoof then walked out of the auditorium.

Samuel looked around the auditorium. He saw that some of the family groups were starting to leave. He looked around and saw that the news crew was still hanging around. He had kept an eye out for them, trying to avoid them. He didn't want to be pestered by that Kathleen Johnson lady. She was always looking for an angle to make the police look bad. Samuel knew if he stayed any longer she would spot him and he would be obliged to an interview.

"That Johnson lady is still here," Samuel said to Stephanie. "I think she's looking for me. I had better get out of here."

"O.K. Chief," Stephanie smiled. "You better leave then. You have work to do."

Samuel gave Stephanie a kiss then looked at Jacob. "Want to come to the station with me son," he said. "I'll get you checked in and introduce you to your watch commander."

"Sure, dad, ah, Chief," stammered Jacob. "Let's go." Jacob gave his mother a kiss and whispered, "This may take some getting used too."

"You'll do fine," she laughed.

Stephanie watched Samuel and Jacob walk away and wondered, as every cops wife, and mother, has for years, will they be home tonight? Stephanie looked at her watch. 10:00 AM. The morning was gone.

CHAPTER EIGHTEEN

❦

Deliver Me, O Lord, From Evil Men

"Take that gun out of your holster, with your left hand, and drop it on the floor," Lucius said, recalling the sheriffs from hundreds of western movies. "This is fun," Lucius thought. "I'm having a blast," as he watched John gingerly remove his revolver from the holster and place it on the ground.

"Alright," Lucius yelled out, pointing his pistol at John and waving the Thompson around the bank. "Everybody get your hands up. Now!"

It suddenly dawned on Lucius that he didn't know what to do next. He had to get some money but he didn't know if he needed to get in the safe. Who would watch all these people while he was in the safe? He laughed suddenly as he thought that he would put everybody in the safe and make them load the money for him.

"Alright," he yelled again. "Everybody, get in the safe."

"The safe is locked," John said.

"Well, open it," Lucius answered.

"I can't. I'm just the guard," John replied, immediately regretting saying that. He hoped Lucius wouldn't try to get one of the other employees to open the safe.

"Who can open it, then," Lucius said getting frustrated. This was supposed to be easy.

"No one can," John said. "It's on a time lock system. It won't open until the prescribed time."

"We'll just have to wait for the prescribed time then, won't we," Lucius said, wondering when that would be. He hoped it wouldn't be a long time. Somebody was bound to come to the bank and see what was going on. This was not going like he had thought it would.

"Why don't you just take the money from the teller window," John advised, hoping Lucius would take the money and leave without hurting anyone.

"Shut up, man! Shut up," Lucius yelled, pointing the Thompson at John. He was losing control. "How much in the window?"

"Two, three thousand," answered John, trying to stay calm. This was his bank, now. Mrs. Riesling and the rest were under his care now.

"That's not enough! I need more," Lucius demanded.

Stephen had been about to exit the lounge when he heard someone yelling. He decided to peek out of the door into the bank to see what was happening. He was shocked to see some young guy, a couple of years younger than himself, holding one of those machine gun he used to see in the old World War Two movies, waving it around as he yelled. He was pointing another gun at John. What's going on, he wondered? Was it one of those mock robberies the cops did to help train the bank staff? The guy with the gun didn't look like a cop. And the cops didn't have those kinds of guns. What's going on? It dawned on Stephen. Unbelievable as it was, he understood. It was a robbery!

Stephen was about to walk out into the bank lobby but something held him back. "The guy doesn't even know that I'm here," he thought. "He doesn't know I'm here! I can hide in the bathroom until he's gone," he thought. "No, I'm the only one who can get help. I have to call for help."

Stephen went to the phone in the lounge and dialed 9-1-1. He looked at the clock. It was 10 minutes after 10 in the morning. He could hear the phone ringing. A gruff but professional females voice answered, "Metropolitan Police, emergency."

While Lucius was trying to figure out how to get more money the police dispatcher broadcast the call of a "bank robbery, occurring now. " She advised responding units that a bank employee still on the line reported that the lone suspect was armed with a sub-machine gun. The first unit arrived within minutes and parked out of sight. The officer maneuvered to where he could see inside of the bank without being seen himself. The officer called in reporting that window tinting made it hard to see into the bank, but he had been able to see one suspect armed with a Thompson M1 sub-machine gun walk past the front bank doors. That officer then co-ordinated other units and within a few minutes the bank was surrounded.

Inside the bank a phone started ringing. Pamela realized for the first time what a slow morning it had been. The phone had not rung once since she had been in the bank. She wanted to answer the phone but was afraid that would give her away as the bank manager. She thought John was handling the situation pretty well. He was the guard after all. Let him face the danger. That's what she paid him for. The phone continued to ring.

"Perhaps I should get that," John suggested.

"Let it ring," Lucius said.

"If we don't answer someone may think something is wrong and call the police," John reasoned.

For the first time in this whole mess Lucius thought of the police. Oh, man! What am I doing, Lucius thought? I should just take the couple of thousand in the teller window and get out of here.

Lucius pointed the pistol in his left hand at Pamela, "You," he said. "Answer the phone. Get rid of them. Tell them you're busy or something."

He jabbed at John with the Thompson. "You, go to the teller window and get me all of the money there," he ordered. "And no funny stuff. I hear the alarm and I'll kill everybody. Hear me!"

"Yes, sir," John said and started towards Kari's window, eyeing his revolver on the ground as he walked past it. John noticed that Stephen was gone. Boy's got sense he thought. He won't do anything stupid.

Lucius followed John to Kari's window. He liked being called sir. It was wonderful what a couple of guns could do for your image he thought. He wondered briefly if he could get the teller to open the other drawers. His thoughts were interrupted.

"Excuse me, sir," Pamela said. Lucius turned to look at her keeping the Thompson pointed at John. "It's for you."

Lucius pointed the pistol at Pamela again. "What do you mean, it's for me?" he screamed. "Who would call me here? Don't play no dumb bank tricks on me. I've got the guns. I'll kill you."

"It's the police department, sir. They want to talk to you," Pamela said, frightened at what reaction that might bring from Lucius.

Lucius wondered how the police knew he was here. Nobody had moved. Nobody had called. Maybe it was just a joke. A distraction. That's what it was. A trick.

"Everybody, get back there. Behind the counter," Lucius ordered. He figured he could get everybody in one place where he could see them all. If it was a trick he could mow them all down with the Thompson. The thought frightened, yet excited him. The idea of killing these people filled him with a feeling of power. He had the power. He was in control.

After everybody got behind the counter he walked over to the desk, keeping the Thompson trained on the employees. He put the pistol in his waistband and picked up the phone.

"Yea," he said.

"Young man," the voice at the other end said. "This is Lieutenant Andrews from the Metropolitan Police Department. Why don't you put your gun down and come on out?"

"Put my gun down?" Lucius asked. "Put my gun down and come out? Why don't you come get me copper?" Lucius was lost now. He was caught and he knew it. Where had he ever imagined this stupid idea anyway? Now here he was relying on old movie lines.

"Son," Andrews pleaded. "Look out side. There's nowhere to go. Why don't you give it up and come on out?"

Lucius looked outside. There were cops everywhere. The Andrews guy was right. He would never get out of there. He was going to go to jail. He couldn't go to jail. He couldn't handle jail. He had heard about jail. He heard what happened to young guys like him. He couldn't survive jail. He wouldn't survive. What was he going to do? How was he going to get out of this mess? Hostages, Lucius thought. I've got hostages!

"Shut up, cop," Lucius yelled. "Shut up. Don't come in here or I'll kill the hostages. I'll kill them all."

"What's your name, son?" Andrews asked trying to change the subject. He didn't want this guy talking about killing anybody.

"What do you want my name for, cop?" Lucius yelled. He was losing control. "What do you want my name for?"

"I want to know what to call you," Andrews answered calmly. He needed to keep this guy under control.

It made sense to Lucius. They needed to call him something. "Lucius," he answered, calmed a little, before thinking he could have given them any name.

"O.K. What are you doing Lucius?" Andrews asked, trying to get Lucius mind off of the situation he was in. Maybe he could talk him out of there.

"I'm robbing a bank!" Lucius yelled, getting excited again. "What does it look like I'm doing?"

"I know Lucius," continued Andrews. "What I want to know is why."

"I needed some money, man," Lucius continued, sounding more out of control than ever. "All I needed was $200. That's all. All I wanted was to go on spring break with my friends. But would my dad help me? No! To tight to part with his money."

Andrews recognized that this was going nowhere. But he had to try. He had to get those people out. He had to get them out safely.

"Lucius, look," Andrews tried. "Why don't you come on out. So far all you've done is tried to rob a bank. No one's been hurt. You'll go to court here locally. No FBI or anything. But if you insist on keeping those people in there, or if anyone gets hurt, it will be out of my hands. You've never done anything like this before have you?"

"Listen, cop," Lucius was calming down and starting to think again. And that made matters worse. "Do you really think it matters whether I go to jail for robbery or murder? Do you really think it matters whether you put me in jail or the FBI does?"

Andrews was not sure where this was going but he didn't like it.

"Yes, Lucius," he answered. "It does. There is a big difference in how much time you will serve in jail. Besides, you don't want to hurt anyone there in the bank. They haven't done anything to you."

"Get off it, cop," Lucius yelled. "I can't do any time in jail. I've heard of those places. I know what they'll do to me. No way man. And these people in here," Lucius continued as he waved the Thompson around the bank. "They haven't hurt me, huh?"

Lucius was really losing control now. "Why do you think all of these people are in here?" Lucius persisted. "They have money. They're either putting some in the bank or getting it out. You think any of them cares that all I need is $200 dollars. That without it I can't go on Spring Break. No, they don't care about me. And I don't care about them. I'm not going to jail. I'm going to kill everybody in here. Then I'm going to kill you."

Andrews looked at his watch. It was 10:30 AM. Only 10:30 in the morning. This was going to be a long day, he thought.

CHAPTER NINETEEN

❧

…the Lord Will Hear When I Call To Him…

SAMUEL FOUND HIS OFFICIAL CAR PARKED IN THE spot reserved for the Chief of Police in the Academy parking lot. He had asked Vanderhoof to have his car brought to the academy since he was riding in from home with Stefy. Whatever Vanderhoof's faults were, he could be counted on to follow instructions. He got in the driver's seat and unlocked the electric door latch, allowing Jacob to get in. Past chiefs had been allowed a driver. Samuel thought that it was a waste of a good cop. He could drive his own car and the driver could be assigned somewhere where he could do some good.

Samuel and Jacob put their seat belts on and Samuel started the car. Immediately the police radios in the Chief's car came on. Being the Chief Samuel felt he needed the ability to contact anyone in the department immediately if needed. He also didn't want to lose the habit, developed over many years in a patrol car, of listening to several radios at once and being able to decipher which operator was giving which information. He also prided himself in being attuned to the sounds of the radio and being able to instantly tune in to most important information.

Samuel backed out of his parking spot and started talking to Jacob, explaining some of the duties of a police officer. Jacob had, of course, heard it all before, but Jacob was not one to ask someone who had infinitely more knowledge than he did to shut up. You never know when you could learn something if you shut up yourself and listen to folks. Samuel had instilled that tenet in Jacob. Jacob believed in it. So he listened. And he learned.

As they were preparing to exit the parking lot Samuel noticed that the departments tactical channel was in use. He wondered what was occurring and tuned his ear to the channel. At the same time his beeper starting vibrating. He kept it on vibrate, instead of chime, again from long years of patrol duty. You didn't want the chime sounding when you were in some dark warehouse looking for some burglar who was hiding in who knows what dark spot. Keep it on vibrate at all times and you'll never forget to turn the chime off on those occasions when you need it off.

Samuel checked the number and saw that it was Vanderhoof's mobile phone. He picked up his phone and started dialing Vanderhoof, keeping the tactical channel tuned in at the same time. While the phone rang Samuel heard officers being routed to assist in forming a perimeter around a certain part of the city and assisting with traffic and crowd control. He could discern that some streets, including a portion of Center St. had been blocked off. Wasn't the bank on Center St? He heard Lt. Andrews on the radio. Besides being the on duty Watch Commander, Andrews was also the department hostage negotiator. If there were a tactical situation, as Watch Commander, Andrews should be in the station handling operations from there. His field sergeants could handle the scene until a command post was set up. If Andrews had been required to come to the actual scene...

"Captain Vanderhoof," answered the voice on the phone.

"Van. Sam here," said Samuel casually. "What's going on?"

"Chief, we've got a situation here," Vanderhoof responded, refusing to let his hair down.

"Tell me about it," Samuel said.

"Some young kid tried to rob the Metropolitan Bank. Armed with what appears to be a Thompson sub-machine gun and an old Colt .45 pistol," Vanderhoof explained.

"Uh huh, go ahead," Samuel urged.

"Well, we got a bank employee who apparently was on break when the crook came in. Called the P.D. Still on the phone with us. Crook doesn't know he's there."

"How's the employee doing," Samuel asked apprehensively.

"Young kid. But there's something to him," Vanderhoof offered. "Prepared to help out in any way he can. Says the crook has rounded up everybody in the bank behind the teller counter. Seems he has taken them hostage. Kid thinks he can stay on the phone with us. Separate line. Doesn't show up on the business phones."

"Good," said Samuel. "Let's keep him on as long as we safely can. Any customers?"

"According to the employee, name of Stephen by the way, there is one other teller, the guard, the bank manager and three other people he figures are customers. He has seen two of them before. The other guy is an older man in a well cut suit."

"So we have three customers, three employees and Stephen for a total of seven hostages. Am I right?" asked Samuel.

"Best as we can tell right now, Chief," answered Vanderhoof.

"Andy?" asked the Chief, referring to Lt. Andrews.

"He's there. Been there for 30, maybe 40 minutes." Vanderhoof paused before relaying the shocking information. "Chief. The crook, a kid who calls himself Lucius, says he isn't coming out because he is afraid of jail. Doesn't trust us. Says he is going to kill the hostages then come out and kill us. Andrews doesn't think the kid is all there. Thinks he will start killing as soon as he works up the nerve. Then he'll come out and commit suicide by cop."

Suicide by cop. Samuel hated that. But it was a fact of life. There were some folks out there who, if they couldn't get their way, if they felt they had been ruined, would ruin you too by forcing your hand. Too many cops had been forced to shoot some idiot who didn't have the courage to pay for his mistakes.

"O.K. Van," Samuel said. "Keep Andy on it. Maybe the kid will come out. I'll be right there."

"We've got a tough one here," Samuel said looking over at Jacob.

"Sounds like it, Chief," Jacob said. "What do I do?"

"For right now just stay with me," Samuel suggested. "It's going to be too hairy a situation to put you out on the perimeter without a training officer. Stay with me. Watch and listen. Maybe you'll learn something."

They drove the rest of the way to the bank in silence. Samuel resisted the urge to go Code-3. Lights and sirens. There was no need for that, really. There were competent officers on the scene already. No sense endangering people with high speed driving. He would get there soon enough. He just hoped there would be something he could do. He didn't want anybody to die today.

〜

CHAPTER TWENTY

And From the Roof He Saw A Woman Bathing…

Kathleen and Stuart had talked to several of the new police officers and their families. They might be able to get some of that the footage in. Kathleen was trying to get some of the new officers to shed a little negative light on the academy experience. Especially from the female officers. Were they treated fairly? Any sexism? Racism? She was disappointed to find none. She was sure the officers had all been brain washed. That's what the academy process was for anyway, wasn't it? To teach all of the new officers to believe in the same things and act the same way? Brain washing. She was also looking for the Chief. She really wanted an interview with him.

"See the Chief anywhere?" Kathleen asked Stu.

"Not right now," answered Stuart. "He was over by the back wall just a few minutes ago."

"Let's take one more quick look for him," Kathleen said. "I sure would like to have an interview with him on this clip. I want to question him about this God in police work business. What about separation of church and state? I've got him this time. Let's find him."

Stuart looked at Kathleen and saw the excitement on her face. For the first time he caught a glimpse of a Kathleen he had never seen. It looked as if there were a little streak of, what, meanness? Evil? She wanted to put a stop to the Chief talking about God. Stuart wondered why. Then Kathleen looked at Stuart and smiled at him. Stuart was again taken by Kathleen's beauty accentuated by her excited state. "Oh, well," thought Stuart. "Let's go find the Chief." He was looking forward to that beer. And maybe dinner.

Kathleen's beeper started beeping. She had forgotten to switch it to vibrate. She was glad it had not gone off while Stu was taping. She checked the number and saw that it was the station. She got her cellular phone out of the equipment bag and dialed the station using one of the preset numbers. The news editor, Mr. Garvey, answered it immediately.

"Hello, what," Garvey answered gruffly.

Kathleen could picture him, sitting in the high backed, overstuffed chair in front of the county map behind his desk. His tie would be undone and his shirt collar unbuttoned. He would have an unlit cigar in his mouth, which he chewed on unmercifully. He could no longer light his cigar in his office since the station had become a smoke free work place, but he refused to take the cigar out of his mouth.

"This is Kathleen, Garv," she announced, switching to her sultry voice. She could usually get over Garvey's gruffness if she put forth just the right combination of sexiness and professionalism. "You rang?"

"Yeah, I did," Garvey answered, getting the tightness in his stomach that he always felt when he spoke with Kathleen. "You still at the academy." He tried to maintain control, to sound authoritative, but he felt it slipping away already.

"Yes, Garv. We've got some good footage. I think you'll like it. Can't wait to show you," Kathleen cooed.

Garvey lost the battle. "O.K. Kat," he said. "But first why don't you and that bum of a camera man get over to the Metropolitan Bank on Center Street. Apparently they've got a bungled robbery attempt. They've got hostages."

Kathleen hated to be called Kat, but she knew she had won Garvey over when he started calling her pet names. "We're on it," she answered and hung up the phone.

Stuart looked at Kathleen inquisitively and she put the phone away. "Bank on Center St., Stu. They've got a robbery working. With hostages." Kathleen was excited.

"Oh, great," Stuart said as he and Kathleen started walking rapidly towards the door. "This should play into the graduation stuff great. Maybe the Chief will be there."

"Yeah," Kathleen added. "Maybe we'll get lucky and catch the cops shooting the crook. Or maybe a hostage will get hurt. Either way it will make a good story."

Stuart looked at Kathleen and saw that look on her face again. For the second time Stuart wondered about her. What drove her? What was her motivation? But as they neared the door a soft draft swept in from the outside, the air blowing a whiff of Kathleen's perfume into Stuart's face. As he caught the soft scent he thought again what a beautiful woman Kathleen was and how lucky he was to be working with her. He certainly was looking forward to that beer.

∽

CHAPTER TWENTY ONE

…I Must Be About My Fathers Business…

IN THE SILENCE THE RIDE SEEMED EXCEPTIONALLY long to Jacob Crue. He had plenty of time to think. Plenty of questions to ask. One look at his father was enough to convince him that now was not the time to ask them. He would watch and listen. Learn something. Help in any way that he could. He was, after all, a cop now.

He thought of everything he had learned in the academy. Of the elements to the various crimes. He tried to remember the code sections involved. Of the different tactics that would be used to try to solve this particular event. Then he thought of the people involved. The fear and uncertainty that the hostages must be feeling. Helplessness. Being held against their will. Unable to do anything about it. Then he thought of all of the forces being brought together to help them. To combat the wrong that was being done. He was amazed. Almost overwhelmed. All it took was one call. Someone needed help and made a call. A call directed to the right place and all of this took effect. His father had a plan. It was implemented right from the beginning.

Jacob looked at his father again and saw the pain. The pain that he suffered when his people, his people, were wronged. He had taken an oath to keep this people safe. And it hurt him when someone tried to hurt them. Now he would right the wrong. Then Jacob realized just how much his father loved these people. Most of them didn't even know him. He was just the Chief. Some vague figurehead to be called upon when needed. Then put back on the mantle piece. Out of the way until he was needed again. Still he loved them. And would give his life for them.

And Jacob knew. Yes, he knew. These were his people, too. And he loved them.

"How're you doing, Stephen?" Lt. Andrews asked, wondering what was going on in this young mans mind.

"Fine, Sir," Stephen answered. "How's it going on your end?"

"We're right on schedule," Andrews said, not knowing what schedule he was talking about. "We'll have you guys out of there in just a short while."

"The sooner the better," Stephen said.

"Right," responded Andrews. "Can you still see this guy?"

"Hold on," Stephen said. "Let me get near the door."

Very slowly Stephen pushed the door open. Just a little. Just enough to see back into the bank proper. He could see most of them. Where was Kari? There she is. Yes, they were all there. And the robber? Where was he? Stephen almost screamed as Lucius walked into his view. Carefully, he let the door close. Lucius had been near the back door somewhere. Mercifully Lucius had not been near when Stephen pushed the door open. Lucius was watching his hostages or Stephen might have been seen.

"He's still there," Stephen said, fighting down a wave of nausea. "He has all of the people in back of the teller counter. Near the back door. Look's like he's walking up and down the bank. Pacing."

"OK. Keep the phone line open," Said Andrews. "We'll be back to you soon."

"Alright," Stephen said. "I'll be right here."

"Where else could I be," he thought, "but right here". He listened at the door and wondered how long it would be until this guy... what was his name, Lucius, that was it...until Lucius started looking around the bank. How long before he decided to look into the other doors. How long before he would be discovered. He had just about been found then. He needed to be a little more careful. But he needed to help the people in the bank, too.

"Courage and wisdom, Lord," Stephen prayed. "Give me courage and wisdom. Help me to help them. Amen." He went looking for a place to hide in case Lucius came into the room.

Chief Crue arrived at the scene and automatically surveyed the area. He noticed the placement of the officers, their cars, the barricades. He noticed that the emergency lights on all of the cars not on the actual perimeter were off. No sense having the lights on if they were not really needed. More of a distraction than an aid. He also noticed that the crime scene was a combination of taking what area the police needed to complete their task while at the same time minimizing the adverse effect on the local business and citizens. The street was blocked off but the detours were clearly marked well in advance. The effect on traffic was minimal. Who ever set up this crime scene was good. Real good. Samuel made a mental note to find out who had done it and comment on it personally.

Samuel's car approached a barricade. The officer on post recognized him and he was allowed into the crime scene. He noticed the interested glance cast into his car as the officer noticed the rookie cop next to Samuel.

"When we get to the command post report to the duty sergeant for assignment", Samuel told Jacob.

"Yes, sir", Jacob responded. He remembered his classes on emergency situations. He would check in with the duty sergeant and receive his assignment. He would check with the logistics officer for whatever equipment he needed and go to his post. When he was relieved he would return his equipment to logistics and check out with the duty sergeant.

Samuel parked his car near the command van. He wanted to tell Jacob so much more. To make sure his first duty would be simple. But he knew that Jacob had received the best training he could be given. He would now have to put that training, and his trust in God, to use.

As Samuel started to exit his car he saw Vanderhoof headed in his direction. He had hoped to get briefed by Andrews but Vanderhoof was the ranking officer. He would do the briefing. Samuel started towards the van. Vanderhoof fell in beside him. Jacob followed. Vanderhoof started explaining the situation as they walked. By the time they reached the van Samuel was up to date on all that was going on.

Samuel surveyed the van. He saw Andrews sitting in the back of the van surrounded by a bank of phones and radios. The nerve center of the van. Here the incident commander had access to virtually anything that could be needed. The phones, they had cellular phones or they could tap into the phone lines, provided land communications. There were radios for the patrol channel, the executive channel, the tactical channel and the fire and paramedic channel. There was also a radio set to the Clemars channel, the statewide emergency police channel. On this they could communicate with any police agency within radio range. Just above eye level was a bank of video monitors. The only one currently operating was connected to a camera on top of the van. It was trained on the front of the bank. The rest could be remotely attached to other video cameras set up where ever they were needed or they could be tuned in to the local television stations.

Seated next to Andrews was the communications officer. This unlucky soul had the unenviable job of operating all of the radios and telephones while keeping at least one eye on the monitors. The job really required at least two, maybe three persons. But space prohibited that. This was manned by an older officer, Rivers. Rivers had never promoted for some reason. But he was sharp. And close to retirement.

The third person in the van, at the mouth of the van really, was the duty officer. Sitting at a small folding table armed with several clipboards was a young Corporal. Corporal Paul Baldwin. Samuel checked in with him then entered the van. The Chief saw Baldwin enter his name and the time on one of the clipboards. Nobody escaped the scrutiny of the duty officer. Lt. Andrews raised his right hand in Samuel's direction in acknowledgment and continued speaking into the phone held in his left hand. Samuel had the urge to grab the phone and talk to who ever was on the other end.

He wanted to get on the radio and start giving commands. He fought off the urge. He knew the men in the van. They were all good. They knew what they were doing. Samuel's job was to supervise. To make the big decisions. And to take the responsibility for what ever happened.

Andrews finished his conversation and put down the phone. "That's our man on the inside," he said." "Still feeding us info. Good guy. I think he'll be alright."

"What do we know about him," Samuel asked. He had a civilian inside that could give them the edge they needed. Or who could get hurt. He hoped the guy was levelheaded and not looking to become a hero. Samuel said a short prayer for the man.

"Not much," Andrews replied. "Young kid, name of Stephen Walsh. A teller. That's about it."

"Can we find out more?" Samuel asked.

"Got a call in to the bank's corporate," Andrews responded. "Waiting on someone from their personnel, uh, human resources department to call us back."

"Good," Samuel replied, not missing the human resources bit. "Any more word on the bad guy."

"Just what I already told the Captain," Andrews said, not sure what Vanderhoof had told Samuel. "Some guy named Lucius holding up the bank. Says he'll kill the hostages before he goes to jail."

Andrews looked at Samuel a moment, then added, "I don't know Samuel. I don't think this guy is all there. I think he's afraid and... well, he's not planning on going to jail."

Vanderhoof cringed at hearing this lieutenant call the Chief by his first name.

"Have we talked to him again?" asked Samuel

"Tried to, Chief," Andrews explained. "He won't answer the phone."

"Keep me up to date," Samuel said. He needed to start planning their options.

"Sure will, Chief," Andrews responded.

Samuel backed away to let Andrews do his work. He wondered about the political pressure being exerted on everyone when, in a crises like this, a man would find the need to use the politically correct phrase or name for some organization or other. Personnel? Human Resources? What difference did it make? He hoped officers were not being influenced by such thoughts in tactical situations.

Samuel turned to Vanderhoof and seeing a news van in the distance figured that news reporters had started to arrive. "How do they hear about these things so fast," he wondered. Then to his dismay he noticed that it was the Channel 3 On The Spot news team. He had dealt with that Kathleen Johnson lady too many times to expect anything good out of her. Samuel didn't know why, but she always tried to put the police in a bad light. No matter what they did. He remembered the slant she put on the Christmas basket deal. Some of the guys identified a few needy families in town, folks they had run across during their normal duties. They gathered toys and a turkey for each family and delivered them on Christmas day. Most of the department got involved in some manner. It was the best Christmas ever for most of the families. And for most of the cops. Seeing the look on the kid's faces as they opened their gifts. The look on the parents faces as they tried to understand what would drive the cops to bring them gifts. The cops feeling of satisfaction that, finally, they had been able to make a difference in somebody's life. Kathleen Johnson reported that the cops were trying to atone for their sins in the community.

Samuel put those thoughts aside. He had work to do. He would deal with the press when the time came. He looked at his watch and saw that it was 10:40 am. Samuel walked out of the command van, signaling Vanderhoof to follow him.

༄

CHAPTER TWENTY TWO

I Believe That You
Are the Christ

ALL EYES WERE ON LUCIUS AS HE PACED BACK AND
forth across the teller windows. Lucius now had the pistol shoved in the
front of his waistband and the Thompson in his right hand. He was trying
to figure out what his next step would be. How he could get out of this.
But he couldn't think. Nothing would work. "They're going to put me in
jail," he thought. "I can't go to jail."

"I can't go to jail," he shouted, pounding on a desk for emphasis. "I
won't go." He looked at the hostages. His hostages. The thought of killing them all came to him again. He felt that surge of excitement again.
A sort of power mixed with fear. As long as he had his guns he had the
power. These people had to do whatever he said. Whatever he wished.
The cops had to listen to him, too. He could do what ever he wanted.
Except leave he remembered. He could not leave the bank. He resolved
that he was going to kill them all. If he couldn't win, then he would hurt as
many people as he could. He would kill them all. But which one first. He
started pacing again.

"Shouldn't you be doing something?" McGuire said to John Nelson. "Get us out of this." McGuire had planned on being in and out of the bank in less than an hour and here it was, what time now? He looked at the wall clock, not wanting to draw attention to his Rolex. It was 10:45 AM.

John looked at McGuire and saw how anxious he was. He saw the expensive suit. The cigars in the shirt pocket. The Rolex watch the man was so obviously trying to hide. John wondered what this man was doing in the bank. A man like this would have someone to go to the bank for him. What was he up to?

"The best thing for us to do right now is to keep quiet and wait for the police," John said. "And pray," he added. Kari looked at John.

"What do you mean, wait?" McGuire said, trying to keep from shouting. "You're the guard. Go do something."

"My duty right now, sir," John said, looking McGuire right in the eye, "is to keep you alive. So I suggest you keep your voice down so as not to attract attention to yourself. And wait for the police."

John looked at McGuire and added, "And pray if you know how."

Kari was sitting in a chair against the wall between the two men. She was afraid. She wished Stephen were here. She wondered where he was. Then she realized it must have been him who called the police. She wondered if he had been able to get out of the bank or if he was still in the break room. She glanced towards the door then quickly turned away. She did not want to direct the robber's attention to the door. In case Stephen was still in there.

Kari's thoughts turned to Stephen and all of the things he had told her. About God. And Jesus. They were the same person but they weren't. She didn't really understand that but Stephen seemed to. She remembered how he told her any number of times not to worry about stuff. God had it under control. He told her that if she could just give it all over to God, give herself to God, she would not have to worry. Well, she was worried. She was scared. But somehow Stephen had been able to call the police.

How did he know to take a break just then? Was that God? And she thought of John right now. He appeared so calm. Was it because of his Navy experience? Because of his age? Or something else? And what had he just said? Pray?

"Oh, God," Kari prayed. "I don't know if you can hear me. I don't know if you even know me. But somehow I believe you are there, that you are listening to me. I don't know how to pray. Teach me. Help me to believe in you. Help me to know you. Like Stephen does."

What am I praying about Kari thought? "God," she continued. "Help us out of this. Save us from this evil man."

Kari noticed that her eyes had been shut tightly. She opened them and found John looking at her. He smiled and winked an eye at her. He whispered, "That's the idea."

Mary Brown was sitting in a corner near the rear of the bank. She was trying very hard to disappear, to become part of the corner. She was also crying. Roger was going to be angry. What was she doing in the bank today anyway, he would ask. Oh, he was going to be angry. She had to get home. She had to get home soon. She had to have dinner on the table. What was she going to do now? How could she explain to Roger why she had been in the bank today? Oh, why did this have to happen today?

Chapter Twenty Three

෧෨

The Wicked in His Pride
Persecutes the Poor

"Come on, Stu," Kathleen rushed. "We're the first one's here. Let's go find the Chief. I'm sure that was him I just saw."

"Just a sec, Kath," Stuart said as he tried to gather his video equipment as fast as he could. "Where did you see the Chief?"

"I think that was him coming out of their van over there," she said, already starting to walk towards the van. "Let's get a statement."

"They're not going to let us in there," Stuart warned.

"We'll get in, Stu. We have work to do," Kathleen said.

Kathleen reached the barricade set up to keep people a safe distance from the bank and to preserve any evidence that might be in the area. With an air of confidence she moved the barricade and started to step around it enjoying the awe with which the small crowd responded to her boldness. An officer stepped in front of her blocking her way. Before the officer could say anything Kathleen grabbed the press pass that she had clipped onto the fine chain around her neck. She shoved it a few inches in front of the officer's face and said simply, "Press."

The officer, a middle-aged veteran with 15 years on the department smiled. "Yes, ma'am," he said. "You can set up anywhere outside of this perimeter. When the press liaison officer arrives I'll let him know that you're here."

Kathleen heard snickers come from the crowd. That angered her. Who did this cop think he was? She was Kathleen Johnson, On The Spot News. She was with the press.

"Officer," she said as if talking to a child. "I don't think you understand. I'm Kathleen Johnson. Channel 3 On The Spot News. I have to get in there to report this incident. Step aside please."

The officer paused for a moment wondering where people like this lady got the idea that they were above the law. Did she think that he stood here in front of a barricade just for the thrill of keeping her from where she was going? He tried to ignore her, hoping she would just go away. He felt her continuing to tug at the barricade.

"Ma'am," he said politely, but sternly. "I believe it is you that doesn't understand. You are not going past this position until it is safe to do so."

"I know, I know," he said, cutting Kathleen off before she could speak. "The press can enter a dangerous area to gather the news, but you cannot enter a crime scene until it is safe to do so. So get your hands off of my barricade and back off."

Now Kathleen was really mad. Who was this guy to tell her to back off? Kathleen glanced over at Stuart, using the opportunity to check out the crowd. To see if they were watching. What their reactions were. Everybody was looking at her. She could not now retreat from this obnoxious officer. She could not admit that the officer was correct. She could not admit defeat. But there was no way she was going to get past the barricade. How could she come out a winner in this situation?

"Officer," Kathleen demanded, "what is your name."

"Boyarski," the officer responded. "Corporal Timothy Boyarski."

"Well," Kathleen said. "I'll be seeing the Chief later today. And you can rest assured he will hear of your rude behavior."

Boyarski did not seem intimidated by her statement. Kathleen looked at the crowd again. They were still watching. Many of them were smiling, laughing at her.

"And Mayor Caton will be hearing from me, also", Kathleen continued, raising her voice to make sure everyone knew she had the last word. "By this time tomorrow you will be looking for another job. Your career here is over."

Kathleen turned on her heel and walked away in a huff. Behind her she could hear some in the crowd laughing.

Kathleen lost that one, she knew, but she wouldn't admit it. She had to console herself that she got in the last word. She didn't get past the barricade, though. She stormed off seeking the comfort of her news van, her domain, bothered by the laughter from the crowd. No wonder everybody hates these cops, she thought. They think they are so high and mighty just because they have a badge and a gun. She would show them. Her hand instinctively reached for her crystal. It comforted her, increasing her strength and resolve.

She saw Stuart standing near the van and cut loose on him. "Thanks for the support, Stu," she said. "Where were you when I needed you? That would have been good footage. Did you see how that cop abused me?"

"Ah," Stu sputtered, thinking that it was Kathleen who had been abusive. "I told you that you couldn't go past there."

"They have no right to keep me out," Kathleen yelled. "I represent the press and I have a right to be in there. The people have a right to know. They want to know. Keep me out will they. I'll show them. They forget the power of the press. We'll see on tonight's news cast."

Stu recoiled at the look on Kathleen's face. They anger made her look almost ugly.

Kathleen released the crystal and looked at Stu, a smile now on her face as she regained her composure. "Let's go find a place to set up before the other crews get here," she said.

Almost ugly. But that smile. "Let's go," said Stu, smitten by Kathleen's beauty again. He again thought of having that beer with Kathleen, but he had seen something about her that left a nagging feeling in his heart. Stu wondered again what drove Kathleen. What her motivations were. The sun glinting off of her hair, the sway of her hips as she walked, almost gliding, towards the passenger door of the van was enough to still his doubts. For now.

CHAPTER TWENTY FOUR

❧

Woe to Men Mighty At Drinking Wine…

FREDO AND HIS FRIENDS WALKED INTO CHARLIE'S Liquor. Fredo could already taste the cold beer. It would help him get rid of the taste in his mouth and the pounding in his head from too much beer last night. As usual, Charlie was standing behind the counter looking at one of the television screens mounted overhead. There were three of them. The first was a monitor for the video camera that pointed at the coolers. Charlie couldn't see the coolers from behind the counter. When he had grown tired of the shoplifters stealing his beer he mounted the camera. Another monitor was for the camera that covered the area from the door to the aisle in front of the cash register, recording the image of everyone coming in. Anyone standing at the register could see him or herself on the monitor. It tended to discourage anyone from robbing Charlie. They knew that once they came into the store, they were on tape. The third screen, flanked by the other two, was larger. It was a standard 13" color television screen. Charlie loved his television. He watched it constantly. Fredo had never been in Charlie's when that television set was not on. And Charlie did not like being disturbed while watching television. You came in, made your purchase and left.

Instinctively, Fredo looked at the screens as he came in.

"Hey, Charlie," Fredo said, familiarly. "What you watching?"

"News," Charlie answered in his usual one-word answers. More often than not you got just a grunt.

Fredo noticed that it was some kind of special report. It was that cute Kathleen what's-her-name from Channel 3. He could see the Center Street sign behind Kathleen. Further back he could see that the street was blocked off. Cop cars were everywhere.

"What they got going, Charlie," Fredo said as he walked past the counter to the beer coolers.

"Robbery," Charlie grunted.

Fredo picked up his beer, deciding on a twelve pack instead of a six. It would take up the rest of his money but maybe he could get some from his dad later. He carried the beer to the counter and set it down. Automatically he looked back up at the TV screen as he waited for Charlie to ring up his beer. Fredo reached a hand into his pants pocket digging for the last of his money.

"What they robbing, Charlie," Fredo asked, playing the age-old game of trying to get Charlie to say more than one word.

"Bank," Charlie said, winning another round.

"No kidding," Fredo said. He looked closely at the scene on the TV and felt his heart sink. He could see the bank in the background. It was the Greater Metropolitan Federal Bank. His dad had walked into the bank just a short while ago. Fredo looked at his watch. It was 10:50 am.

CHAPTER TWENTY FIVE

❧

No, In Your Heart
You Work Wickedness

MARY BROWN WAS SOBBING AUDIBLY NOW. SHE CON-
tinued to try to hide in the corner. She was afraid of the wild looking boy
with the guns. She was afraid of the boy. She was afraid of his guns. She
was afraid of everybody in the bank. But mostly she was afraid of Roger.
She had to get out of here and get home before Roger found out. How
could she keep this from him? Roger was going to find out. Then he
would be angry. He would be very angry. Mary didn't like it when Roger
became angry. Maybe if she talked to the boy with the guns. If she told
him about Roger, he would understand. No. He wouldn't. He wouldn't
care. All she could do was wait and hope that Roger never found out.
Hope. That's all. Mary didn't have much hope.

Lucius was startled by the sudden ringing of the phone. He just stared at
it for a moment then, making a decision, he went over and picked it up.

"I told you guys to leave me alone," he yelled, thinking he was talking to
the police.

He heard a soft, feminine voice on the phone say, "Hello. This is not the police." Lucius recognized the voice but couldn't place it.

"Well then, who is it?" he yelled again.

"It's Kathleen Johnson. Channel 3 On The Spot News?" she announced making it seem almost a question. "I would like to talk to you about what you're doing there."

"I don't want to talk to you," Lucius said, somewhat softer, recognizing the name. "Why would I want to talk to you?"

"Well, I am preparing a report for the evening news," Kathleen said, "and everybody will want to know what is going on here. They'll want to know who you are and why you are doing this."

"I don't care what everybody wants to know," Lucius yelled. Then he started thinking. The evening news. All of his friends would see him. His dad would see him, too. He could tell them, tell them all, how his dad wouldn't give him money. How he was forced to rob banks because his dad was so cheep. If only his dad had given him the money none of this would have happened. Yeah! He would talk to the news.

"Sir," Kathleen said, pretending to let Lucius be in charge. She found that men will cooperate more if you let them believe they're in charge. "Sir, what made you do this? Can you tell me?"

"You're from the news, huh?" Lucius said. "Sure. I can tell you. I'll tell you all about it." Lucius then went on to tell Kathleen about all of the evils that had been directed against him by his father. How deprived he was. How his father failed to support him, financially or otherwise.

"All I wanted was some money to go on spring break," he started. "That's all I wanted. All of my friends were going. Their parents let them go. I asked my dad for $200 so I could go. I never ask him for anything. And he won't give me the money. What was I supposed to do? He wouldn't give me the money." Lucius was ranting now. "If he had just given me the money I wouldn't be here now. These people wouldn't be here. Dad and his precious money."

He forgot to mention the job he had quit. Or what his intentions were at spring break. Of course, Kathleen did not probe those areas. It was a much better story as Lucius was telling it. How the boy had gone bad because of the poor treatment his father gave him. That was a story. There was no sense digging at the cause of the problem. She would report the story. The world would hear. They would recognize the boy's plight as she reported it. This young man had become a criminal because his father wouldn't support him. Probably some old fashion outdated disciplinarian father who probably had even spanked this young boy. Maybe she could interview the father also.

Lucius went on raving about his father. It encouraged his rage. His new found hatred for his father built. He kept imagining new wrongs. The more he told Kathleen the more he believed himself. The more he believed himself the grater his rage. The truth no longer mattered. He was manufacturing his own truth and he liked it much better.

Finally he blurted out, "There's no reason for me to live. My own father hates me," he said. "He would never admit this is his fault. He'd rather let me go to jail. And I can't go to jail."

"What are you saying?" Kathleen asked, sensing even more sensational-ism. What was this kid going to do?

Lucius thought about it for a minute. What was he saying? What was he talking about? What could he do now? He would make his father sorry. That's what he would do. He'd show his father.

"I'm not going to jail," Lucius said. "I'm not coming out. I've got these people in here. They're mine. The cops want them. They can come and get them."

Still fishing for sensationalism Kathleen asked, "Are you going to hurt them?" She never once thought whether she might be giving the boy ideas.

"Hurt who?" Lucius asked.

"The hostages," Kathleen said. "Are you going to hurt them?"

The idea was planted. Lucius liked it. He liked the power he felt. He was in charge. He was in control. He had the power of life and death over all of these people. He controlled the police. They couldn't come in after him. He was going to be on television, in the newspapers. All his friends at spring break would see him. He would be famous.

"Yea," Lucius blurted. "I'm going to kill all of them. I'm not going to jail. And nobody's walking out of here. Either the police leave and let me go, or everybody dies. "

Mary Brown lost all control and starting crying, a strange drawn out wail punctuated by gurgling sobs.

Meanwhile Pamela was wondering how she would explain this to her bosses. What would she tell them? How had she lost control of her bank?

Richard wondered what Fredo was doing and what he would do once Richard was gone. 'He'll wind up in jail again,' Richard thought.

McGuire wondered if he could somehow bribe this kid. What could he offer this kid to let him go? Money? He had plenty of that. And that's obviously what the kid came in here for. But, how much would the kid want? And there was no way the police were going to let this kid go. Maybe they would catch him. Then any money he gave the kid would have been wasted. He would wait on that. Wait until there was no other way.

John looked around at everyone. He saw the hate on Lucius face. Worse, he saw despair. Lucius didn't know, wouldn't know, even if told, he would never know the Truth. Still, he should try. Or should he? He looked at all of the bank employees and customers. He was responsible for their safety. It was them he had to think of. He had to do something. He could try to take Lucius. He did have that Navy training. But, no, that was years ago. He no longer had the same reflexes, the same strength. He would be no match for the much younger Lucius. What could he do? He looked over at Kari. Kari seemed to have found a new strength. She was sitting on the floor now with her back to the wall, holding Mary Brown's hands as Mary sobbed uncontrollably. Kari's lips moved as she spoke soothing words to Mary. No. She wasn't speaking to Mary. Kari saw John looking at her and smiled. Kari smiled back as if she was unafraid. Watching her, John understood. He remembered, also. He remembered when he first met Him. The fire that welled up inside of him. How he instantly knew the answer to every fear. Kari wasn't talking to Mary. She was talking to God. She was praying. Kari was praying. But did she know who she was praying to, he wondered?

John smiled back at Kari. He remembered the long talks Kari had been having with Stephen. He relaxed visibly. John leaned back against the wall and started doing the best thing he could to protect these people. He started praying, also. It was out of his hands, he knew. But not out of His hands.

Meanwhile, Kathleen had her story. She had breaking news. If this kid killed any hostages, it was she who would have the story. If the police went in to get the kid, she would have that story. Either way, she came out the winner. She was on her way to an anchor position. She could feel it.

Stephen had been peeking out of the door. He could only hear one side of the conversation. He didn't know who Lucius was talking to but it didn't sound like he was talking to the police. Stephen thought he better find out. It sounded like Lucius intended to kill everybody in the bank and the police should probably know about that.

Stephen picked up the phone, hoping someone would be there. "Hello?" he asked. "Hello?"

"Yes, hello Stephen," he was answered. "We're here." Stephen recognized Lt. Andrews' voice. It was somehow comforting.

"Was that you guys that were just talking to this guy in here?" Stephen asked.

"No, son," came the reply. "We haven't talked to him in," Andrews looked at his watch, it was 11:15 AM, "about 15 minutes."

"Oh," said Stephen, not knowing how to say this. "Well, he was just talking to somebody on the phone. He got real excited."

"Who was he talking to?" asked Andrews. Lt. Andrews looked around the room to get somebody's attention. "Go get the Chief," he ordered into the room when nobody looked his way.

"I don't know," Stephen answered. "But he told them, ahh, he told them he was going to kill everybody."

Andrews was worried but he didn't want to scare the kid. Where had he heard this? Who was Lucius talking to? How were they able to talk to Lucius?

"You're certain that's what he said?" Andrews asked.

"Yea," Stephen answered. "I heard a phone ring so I looked into the bank. I saw him talking on it. He was saying something about his father and money. Then he said that he was going to kill everybody. Those were his words. 'I'm going to kill everybody'".

"He say anything else?" Andrews asked, looking for a clue as to who the caller was.

"Oh, yea," Stephen remembered. "He said, asked actually, if they were from the news."

"Did he mention which news?" Andrews continued, still looking for that clue.

"No," Stephen answered slowly, trying to remember the conversation. "He just said they were from the news."

"Alright, Stephen," Andrews said. "Did the other people hear him?"

"I think so," Stephen answered, wondering if they were all as scared as he was. "They're a lot closer to him than I am".

"Are they all OK?" Andrews hoped.

"Yeah, except for this one lady," Stephen said. "Mrs. Brown I think her name is. A regular customer. She's crying real bad."

"Alright Stephen," Andrews said, trying to sound confident. "We'll have you guys out of there real soon. Now stay out of sight. We'll keep the line open."

"Alright," Stephen said. "I'll be right here." He regretted that as soon as he said it. Sounded too flippant, and he definitely didn't feel that way.

CHAPTER TWENTY SIX

❧

…not Willing That Any Should Perish…

SAMUEL RUSHED INTO THE VAN, LOOKING FOR Andrews. "What's going on," he asked.

"Somebody, probably a news crew sounds like, got a call into the bank." Andrews reported. "They talked to our bad guy. Our guy on the inside heard the conversation. One side of it anyway."

Andrews paused, actually afraid to report the rest. "The bad guy told them he's going to kill everyone."

"What news crew?" Samuel asked.

"We don't know," Andrews said.

"Any local news shows on now?" Samuel asked. "Turn on one of the monitors."

Rivers flicked at a bank of switches and one of the monitors came to life. Another switch and the blank screen came alive with images of a beautiful, perfectly attired and coifed woman arguing with a middle aged

86

man while a middle aged woman eaves dropped from the other side of a door in what was obviously a daytime soap opera. Rivers moved a dial and the images on the screen changed as he flipped through the channels. There were no news shows on.

"Nothing, Chief," said Rivers.

"Thanks," Samuel replied. "What time is it?"

"11:25," Rivers answered.

"Sir," he continued. "Channel 3 has an 11:30 news show."

"They're outside," Samuel said. "It's that Kathleen Johnson lady."

"Yes, Sir," Rivers said. "One of the posts reported having a little run in with her."

Samuel shook his head slowly. "Keep an eye on three, then," he said. "Let's see what Johnson makes of this. I hope it wasn't her talking to this kid."

Rivers had already turned the dial. On the screen someone was pouring an exact line of mustard, which poured unerringly from the tip of the mustard bottle, on to a perfectly colored hotdog while in the back ground a father and son tossed a soft ball back and forth as they played a game of catch. Abruptly the scene changed and a half dozen more hotdogs were shown grilling on a perfectly clean gas barbecue grill.

Vanderhoof looked at Samuel as if deciding whether or not he should speak. Samuel was watching the TV monitor without actually seeing it. He was deep in thought.

"Chief," Vanderhoof said. "We could send in the Special Tactics Unit. There is access from the front. They could be in very quickly."

Samuel looked at Vanderhoof, grunted and nodded for Vanderhoof to continue.

"They would have to rush across the Plaza, probably come in from the parking lot."

Samuel was listening. As a Lieutenant, Vanderhoof had spent some time as the Special Tactics Unit Commander. He knew how it operated and what its capabilities were.

"Once inside they could quickly locate this Lucius fellow and neutralize him," Vanderhoof continued, remembering, from long practice, to use innocuous words at strategic points. "With our fellow on the inside we would have a pretty good idea where he was before we made entry, maximizing our chance for success."

Samuel sighed and crossed his arms as he walked across the trailer, deep in thought. He ran his left hand across his face, starting at his forehead and ending with his chin in his hand. He massaged his chin for several seconds then looked up at Vanderhoof. He was looking for holes in the plan. If there were holes, anything that could go wrong, he had to know how to plug them. Every plan had holes. If the holes could be effectively plugged, then it was a workable plan. If the holes could not be plugged, or if plugging the holes created other holes, the plan was not workable.

Hole number one. Crossing the open Plaza in front of the bank.

"How long would it take the team to get across the Plaza?" Samuel asked.

"Fifteen, twenty seconds at the most," Vanderhoof replied, elated that his plan was being considered.

"Long time," Samuel said.

"As long as the team keeps moving they are not a very good target," Vanderhoof replied, closing a hole. He had listened to the Chief talk about overcoming holes on many occasions and had learned to expect them to be exposed. He had learned to fill the holes.

"Van," Samuel said. "Have you ever been inside of that bank?"

"Never," Vanderhoof answered, simultaneously wondering, where this was going and thinking that he would not be seen in this bank. He did his banking at American Bank, in the affluent east side of town. He was about to suggest they could find a blue print for the building.

"I have," Samuel continued. "It's not a large bank. In fifteen to twenty seconds you can walk from the front door to any other part of the bank. Does that present us with any problems?"

Vanderhoof nodded slowly, trying to hide his embarrassment as he thought he saw the hole and tried to find a plug. He couldn't. "On any forced entry we have a chance of violence, Chief," Vanderhoof covered. "That's why we use the Special Tactics Unit. They are heavily armed and have body armor. I don't think he has anything that can hurt us."

"Exactly," Samuel said. "When he sees the Special Tactics Unit coming, he knows he can't stop them, or he tries to and finds out he can't, so what does he do? What is his only hope of stopping us?" Samuel looked at Vanderhoof, not really expecting an answer. He continued, "He starts taking out civilians. How do we stop that?"

Having been a Marine, Samuel knew the military mind set. It was the military that had devised many of the tactics that special weapon and tactics units around the world used today. The difference between the military and police work was that the military accepted casualties. In police work you didn't. You hoped that you didn't have to shoot the bad guy. You did what you could to avoid getting a cop hurt. But how could you justify losing a civilian?

Vanderhoof was hurt. He had stopped his planning with the entry. He figured they would have to take the bad guy out to stop him from hurting anyone inside. He never imagined that the shooting could start before the team got there. He had thought of his Tactical Unit being shot at but the idea of the hostages being injured had not crossed his mind. Still, they had to get the robber in order to get the hostages out. And no plan was perfect.

"If we move fast," Vanderhoof continued, "we can keep the damage to a minimum. If we get word in to the guy inside, maybe he can get the others to spread out. That way this Lucius kid can only get to one or two before we get him."

"Those are our people in there, Van," Samuel said. "We're here to protect them. I'm not willing to lose any of them."

"We'll probably lose Lucius," Van said.

"He has a choice, Van," Samuel said. "He doesn't have to die. He has to make a choice. I can't make it for him. I don't want to lose him either but he alone can make that choice."

CHAPTER TWENTY SEVEN

~

Give no Regard to Mediums Or Familiar Spirits

KATHLEEN HUNG UP THE PHONE, DROPPING IT INTO her handbag as the idea formed in her mind. Automatically her right hand reached for the crystal hanging from her neck. She rubbed it gently, but firmly, trying to draw power from it, to meld herself with the earthly powers being channeled through the crystal. She had to clear her mind so that the power of the cosmos could enter and help her to develop the idea. Immediately the thoughts started forming, almost as if someone were speaking to her.

"Stu," she yelled as she reached into her bag for the cell phone. "Find us a good spot to work from. We're going to go live at 11:30."

Stuart looked at Kathleen in amazement as he subconsciously scanned the area trying to visualize a live shot. What did she have up her sleeve this time, he wondered?

Kathleen pulled her cell phone from her purse and dialed the station number quickly. "Put Garvey on, quick," she said as soon as the phone was answered. "It's Kathleen," she huffed to the voice on the other end, the owner of which had the audacity to question her identity. A few seconds later she was discussing her plan with Garvey.

"Garvey," she said, not worrying about trying to seduce him with her voice. Garvey was a newsperson. The news would be seduction enough. "I made a phone call to the bank. I talked to the robber. A kid..."

"You did what?" Garvey yelled.

"I talked to the bank robber," she continued. "I got his story."

"How in all get up did you manage that?" Garvey asked, not sure he wanted to know.

"I just called the bank and the guy answered," she said. "I guess he was expecting the police to call because he just answered."

"What have you got?" Garvey asked, getting interested. "Is it any good? Can we use it?"

"It appears the kid's father doesn't support the kid," Kathleen started. "The kid, his name is Lucius, is flat broke. This morning Lucius asked his father for some money and the father turned him down. He had no where else to turn." She conveniently left out the spring break part.

"Sounds like some kind of a sob story," Garvey said.

"Human Interest, Garvey", Kathleen said. "This kid sounds like he was desperate. He is desperate. He says he is going to kill his hostages. He doesn't want to go to jail. We have the exclusive on this Garv."

"Kill the hostages? He said that," Garvey asked. "OK. What do you have in mind?"

"I'd like to go live at 11:30," Kathleen said. "Stu is already setting up the shot. We could start with a report on the robbery then I could add the interview for Human Interest."

Garvey thought about it. Saying the kid was going to kill the hostages was probably not a real good idea, considering the hostage's families. Still, no one else had the story. They were still the only news crew at the bank. This story would be talked about for days. And all stories would lead back to Channel Three's interview with the crook. That clinched it.

"Go with it," Garvey said.

"I love you, Garv," Kathleen said, beaming, and switched off the phone.

Back in the Command Trailer the television monitor scene changed once again. The logo for the Channel Three On The Spot News appeared on the screen. The visage of the anchorman faded in as a voice started over the familiar jingle. It announced the 11:30 version of the On The Spot News. It introduced Michael Hale, the anchorman. The camera panned to the right to show the face of a dark haired woman with an impossible smile. She was introduced as Caryn Dirkes-DiSalvo, the co-anchor. The scene then changed to an athletic looking man in a well-tailored suit. He would report all the up to the minute details on the sports scene. The anchorman reappeared and announced that Channel Three On The Spot News would also be presenting breaking news. Dirks-DiSalvo took over and announced that Kathleen Johnson was on the scene of a take over robbery at one of the local banks and had been following the story.

The scene changed again and there stood Kathleen, the bank in the distant background, a police officer manning a barricade directly behind her.

"That's right," Kathleen said. "And we will tell you why this robbery is occurring including details from my exclusive interview with the alleged robber."

The scene changed back to the anchors. Michael Hale said, "All of this and more after these brief commercials."

Again the scene changed. A familiar jingle started. A dimly, although gaily, lit room filled with extremely beautiful women and physically fit men appeared. Everyone in the room was laughing or dancing, carefree. Each was holding a frosty looking bottle of the leading brand of beer. A manly sounding voice advertised the virtues of this particular beer. If you drank this particular beer, you too could laugh and dance with beautiful men and women in a carefree world it seemed to proclaim as a woman in painted on pants and a barely there blouse threw her had back and laughed as a young man wrapped his arms around her waist and spun her around the dance floor.

Everyone in the van looked at the Chief, knowing that this news could not forebode well. Not if it was coming from Kathleen Johnson.

CHAPTER TWENTY EIGHT

∽

…His Only Begotten Son…

SEVERAL EXTREMELY BEAUTIFUL, IMPOSSIBLY SLENDER women wearing a variety of revealing athletic wear moved rhythmically across the television screen in a well choreographed dance as loud music with a hypnotic drum beat pounded the rhythm to a woman singing about dancing the night away. All the while a male voice proclaimed the virtues of the American Dream Gym. The gym scene faded and the Channel Three On The Spot News jingle filled the van. All eyes turned towards the monitor above the communications console. The anchors appeared again. Michael Hale started, "Welcome to the Channel Three On The Spot News 11:30 news hour. We have breaking news."

Caryn Dirkes-DiSalvo took over. "There has been a foiled robbery at the Greater Metropolitan Bank on Center Street," she said. "The suspected robber is still in the bank and has apparently taken hostages. Our roving reporter, Kathleen Johnson, is on the scene and has an exclusive interview with the suspect. Kathleen?" Both anchors turned to face a video screen on which was the image of Kathleen Johnson, microphone at the ready, standing in front of a police barricade, the Greater Metropolitan Federal Bank in the distant background.

"Thank you, Caryn," Kathleen started, looking concerned as if the robbery touched her personally. "This morning, apparently right after opening, the Greater Metropolitan Federal Bank, right here on Center Street, was visited by a young man with a mission. A young man, calling himself Lucius Ward, entered the bank with the intention of leaving with enough money to carry him through this spring break weekend. Before he could complete the robbery, police were summoned and they surrounded the bank, spoiling his plans. Lucius, who is allegedly armed with a pistol and a sub-machinegun, has taken the bank employees, and apparently some customers, hostage and is refusing to come out."

"Although police officers are everywhere," Kathleen continued, "we have not been able to get a statement or any information from the police department. Officers have, in fact, refused to allow us to get any closer to the bank or access to the police command post which is about 100 feet to my left." Kathleen indicated an area to her left rear. The scene changed as Stewart moved so that Kathleen's background, originally the bank, was replaced by the police command trailer.

"Trying to get further information," Kathleen said, now looking somber, "I called the bank. I was able to speak to Lucius Ward, the alleged robber. I asked Lucius why he resorted to robbery. He told a story that is all too familiar today. A story of neglected youth. Of parents not willing to care for their children."

"Lucius told me that he was in need of some money," Kathleen continued. "Just a small amount of cash just to get him through the weekend. He asked his father for the money. His father refused to come to his son's aid, leaving Lucius with the dilemma, how to come up with the money he needed. Faced with no job and no other way to raise the money, Lucius was forced to resort to robbery."

"Picture this young man now, if you can," Kathleen said, concern reappearing on her face. "Unemployed and penniless, forced to commit a robbery and suddenly surrounded by police. His immediate future suddenly looks bleak. A lot bleaker than it did a few hours before. The future he is now facing is several years in jail. Lucius fears spending time in jail, as any young man should."

"What Lucius said to me is, 'I'm not going to jail and nobody's walking out of here,'" Kathleen said. "This desperate young man does not intend to go to jail and apparently intends to kill his hostages. We will have to wait and see what the police will do. In their attempts to capture this young man will they neglect to try to get the hostages out safely? We just hope that they don't do anything rash to force this young mans hand and aggravate an already tense situation. Caryn?"

The scene changes back to Michael and Caryn in the newsroom. "Thank You, Kathleen," Caryn says facing the monitor. Turning towards the camera Caryn advises the television audience, "We'll keep you posted as incidents develop."

"Also in today's news," Michael continued, unconcernedly, "Datatrends, the computer software mega-store, is back in the courts..."

Harold Ward had just walked back into the house, habitually turning the television on as he walked past it. He put his package on the kitchen table as the television news droned on about some bank being robbed. As if robberies were news any more, Harold thought. He heard that pretty Kathleen Johnson lady start talking and suddenly stopped what he was doing. Did he just hear her say Lucius Ward was in the bank? He walked to the television and stood, transfixed. Lucius was getting his own money. Or he was trying to.

"Did she really say that on T.V.?" asked Vanderhoof. "I can't believe she actually gave out that information on live television. What if the families of any of the hostages are listening? Didn't she think of that?"

"Apparently not," said Samuel, forcing from his mind the thought that Vanderhoof had also failed to think of the hostage's just short minutes before. "Well, it sounds like she is the one that talked to him. He says he's not coming out and that the hostages are not coming out either. Somehow we have to get them out of there."

"We'll keep your plan in mind, Arthur," Samuel told Vanderhoof. "Have the unit ready in case we need to use them. But I have another idea."

"If we send in the Special Tactics Unit," Samuel said slowly, "The kid will see us coming and may panic. If he panics he may start shooting the hostages right away."

Samuel surveyed the faces of the listening officers, then continued, "According to Stephen, our guy inside, all of the hostages are seated against a wall." Samuel paused to let the picture settle in everyone's mind. "He could hurt a lot of people before we even get to the door," he finished.

Slowly, as if trying out the idea on himself as well as on the others, Samuel continued, "If, however, we send one officer to the door, one uniformed officer, the kid may come to the door."

"If he does, if he comes out, we may be able to arrest him," Samuel said hopefully, less than half believing it would happen. "If he does not come out, but we have reached the door," Samuel looked slowly at each person in the room, "then the officer at the door can engage the kid. The kid would be forced to meet with the officer. He will have to fight the officer. He won't be able to go after the hostages while the officer is there. This will give the hostages inside a chance to escape before he can start shooting at them."

Everyone looked at Samuel incredulously. Samuel inhaled deeply, slowly let out the breath, then continued, "O.K. Here is my plan."

Samuel went on to explain, "When we talk to Stephen again, we tell him to be prepared for our guy coming to the door. When Lucius, that's the crooks name, right?"

"That's correct, Sir," Andrews replied.

"When Lucius is distracted, Stephen has to alert the hostages to our plan. The front door and back door are not in line. The hostages are near the back door." Samuel paused.

Catching on to the idea, Andrews picked up, "When our officer engages the kid, Stephen can lead the hostages safely out through the back door."

"Exactly," said Samuel. "If the kid turns from the officer to get to the hostages, the officer would put him down. So, the kid has to concentrate on the officer."

"What if the bank robber doesn't come to the door?" Vanderhoof questioned.

"Then the officer engages him through the door," Samuel answered. "If the kid goes for the hostages, the officer has to put him down."

They all exchanged glances. The plan sounded good. But there was a hole in it. And everyone in the trailer was slowly finding the hole. Each in turn looked at the Chief, knowing he could not have missed such an obvious hole in his plan. Or had he? Shortly, Samuel found that everyone was looking at him expectantly.

"Everybody see the hole?" Samuel asked.

After a short pause, while everybody stared wide-eyed at the Chief, Vanderhoof responded. "Yes, Sir," he said. "Which ever officer goes in is likely to get hurt."

"Actually," Samuel said, "if the kid inside doesn't give up, the officer that approaches that door is going to die." Samuel looked at all of the faces staring back at him, the obvious shock and disbelief in their eyes.

Samuel continued, "The officer that goes in cannot hide or try to protect himself. If he goes for cover," he explained, "the kid has the chance to go after the hostages. We have to avoid that. The whole point of this operation is to get those people out of there safely. We have to save those people. So the officer has to make himself the obvious target."

Vanderhoof and Andrews stared at Samuel as if frozen in time while Rivers stared at his monitor screens, each of their minds rebelling, refusing to grasp the immensity of what Samuel was saying, even as they heard him say it.

"The only question," Samuel continued, "is who do we send? Who'll go?"

Vanderhoof recoiled as if he had been punched in the chest. He looked at Samuel like the Chief was a ghost that had suddenly appeared before them. He can't be serious, Vanderhoof thought. Yet he could see that the Chief was serious. Vanderhoof came to the realization, for the first time, that Samuel actually loved the people that he was sworn to serve. He understood that the Chief was willing to sacrifice one of his own officers to save a group of citizens. Vanderhoof's chest puffed up a little in pride of his Chief, then puffed up considerably more as he thought, now that the idea had been broached, that he would do the same thing. He also thought of the medals that would be pinned to his chest if he sacrificed an officer to save the citizens. He wondered how he could ensure that he got a medal out of this. His attention to the situation at hand wavered as his mind was overtaken by daydreams of the men being lined up in full dress uniform as the Mayor, or the Governor himself, pinned a medal to his chest as cameras clicked and flashed, video cameras whirred, newscasters sounded his name to countless of watchers sitting in front of television sets across America, a flag draped coffin in the back ground.

"Maybe I should go," Samuel said.

This snapped Vanderhoof's attention back to reality. What if he was asked to go, he thought in horror?

Andrews, sensing the pain his Chief was going through presenting that idea, involuntarily took a step towards Samuel, mentally reaching out to him, knowing that the Chief was prepared to go himself if it would save a citizens life.

Rivers, the junior officer in the room, understood the point the Chief was making all too clearly. He looked away from the monitors, wondering who would make the sacrifice, who would risk sure death, to free a bunch of people he had never seen. The thought of going himself crossed his mind but he knew immediately the plan would never work if he went. He knew that he would revert to his training, his instinct to stay alive, to use cover, avoid direct confrontation, which would allow the suspect to attack the hostages. He had risked his life many times for people he did not know but he knew he was not prepared to intentionally give his life for them.

Who would go?

"Dad," came Jacob's voice from just inside the door of the trailer. Jacob had been standing just outside of the Command Trailer door. Hoping to learn something on his first day at work, he had been watching and listening to everything going on. He listened to the planning going on, feeling the tension in the trailer grow, watching the expressions on each of the faces, seeing their reactions.

Jacob had never known a day when his father was not a policeman. He had grown up in a police household. He had seen the sacrifices that Samuel had made to serve his community, those he had sworn to protect. They were Samuel's people. And he loved them. He would do what ever it took to protect them, he loved them that much. Although he had never met the great majority of them, Jacob knew that his father felt as if he knew each one personally, by name. As if he had been invited to each of their homes and dined with them. As if each was a close part of his family. He loved them that much. Jacob loved them, too. He could not explain it to himself, much less to anyone else, but he loved them. That is why he chose to follow in Samuel's footsteps, because he loved them as if they were his own. He used to see himself as a sheep in a meadow surrounded by ravenous wolves. The only thing that kept the wolves from him was the shepherds, men like his father and those that worked with him. Those that dared to stand between the sheep and wolves, using their lives and bodies to keep the innocent from death, and worse. And now they were his sheep. He was the young shepherd and he had to protect them from the wolves.

"Dad, I'll go."

All eyes turned to Jacob. They had all forgotten he was there. All except Samuel.

Samuel looked at Jacob. "You love them, don't you, son," Samuel said.

"Yes, Dad", Jacob answered. "I do."

Samuel watched Jacob for several long seconds then nodded his head slowly, knowingly. "Okay, son", Samuel replied. "You go."

It was 12 o'clock.

Chapter Twenty Nine

In The Lord I Put My Trust

STEPHEN OPENED THE DOOR JUST A CRACK, VERY slowly, and peered carefully into the bank. Almost immediately he saw Lucius sitting at the loan manager's desk, his back to Stephen. Scanning the room he could see the others sitting on the floor, their backs against desks or cabinets along one wall. He looked for Kari. Her eyes were closed and her lips were moving. It looked as if she were praying. John, the security guard, was looking at Lucius. Mrs. Riesling, his boss, was staring angrily at John, wringing her hands. One of the customers, the older gentleman in the business suit, appeared to be asleep, although he was sweating profusely. The female customer, Mrs. Brown, was crying quietly but uncontrollably. And the customer, Mr. Copas was it? He was sitting staring at Mrs. Brown.

Stephen looked back at Kari, again thinking how beautiful she was. He knew he had to get her out. He had to get them all out. He was the only one who could, he thought.

"Oh, God, My precious Lord," he prayed. "Show me how, Lord. Show me how."

He went back to the phone. A glance at the clock as he went past told him he had been in the bank for three and a half hours. He picked up the phone and spoke softly to see if anyone was on the line. Officer Rivers was on the other end.

"We'll be getting you out of this shortly buddy," Rivers told Stephen. "Hold on, I'll let you talk to Lieutenant Andrews. He'll fill you in on what's up."

Everyone looked expectantly at Rivers when he started talking. Andrews started towards him to take the phone, wondering how he was going to explain this to Stephen. How he was going to understand what was going on. Heck, he's only a kid, Andrews thought. How can I expect him to understand the importance of what we are going to ask him to do? How is he going to carry that out? How will he let the people inside know what they have to do? So many questions, Andrews thought. Out of the corner of his eye he saw Jacob and remembered that he was only a kid also. He noticed how calm he was. Although he had worked with Jacob's father for over 20 years, he never really understood all of the Jesus stuff Samuel stood for. He knew Samuel believed in it. He knew it worked for him. Now, here in the middle of this crisis, with all of these lives depending on them, he thought he began to understand it. Samuel had once told him that the entire Bible, all of God's word could be summed up in one word. Love, Samuel had said. Just one word.

As Andrews reached the phone his thoughts went to years past when his mother and father would take him to the local church. He went to Sunday School while they went to service in the church proper. He remembered the people who had spent so much time trying to get him to understand, what was that they called it, scripture? It had never made much sense to him but they were wonderful stories. The stories flooded back to him now. Who was that man who was going to sacrifice his own son at God's command? What was that he had said, the Lord will provide Himself a sacrifice. Then suddenly there was the sheep caught in the bush that he used for the sacrifice. He remembered the parting of the Red Sea when Moses took the people out of Egypt. He remembered the thief on the cross. Jesus on the cross. His eyes were suddenly opened and he understood that God always took care of His people. He loved His people. For the first time since those Sunday school days, Andrews prayed.

"Lord, forgive me," he said softly. "I've been away. I'm back now. Help me."

He took the phone. "Stephen," he said. "Here's the plan. Listen carefully."

He went on to explain to Stephen what they were going to do and what Stephen needed to do. Andrews told Stephen, "We're going to have an officer come to the front bank doors. That should distract Lucius. While Lucius is distracted Stephen, I need you to get all of the hostages out of the back doors as quickly as you can. You'll have to move fast and keep them moving, no matter what happens. No matter what you see or hear. You keep them moving."

"Can you get them out, son," Andrews asked.

Stephen was thinking. An idea suddenly popped into his head. Immediately he knew that his prayers had been answered. God was in this. He knew it.

"Yes," he exclaimed, maybe a little more excited than he should have been. He had just remembered that Kari had been teaching his some kind of sign language. She had a deaf aunt or something and he had been learning it during their breaks in case a deaf person came in the bank. It was really an excuse to be near her, to have something in common. "Yes, I can."

"Relax, son," Andrews said, nervous at Stephens sudden excitement. He hoped Stephen wasn't some hot shot who was going to get them in trouble while trying to be a hero.

"No, I'm fine," Stephen said, trying to control his excitement. "I don't know if you'd understand it but I just prayed for a way out. I believe in God, Sir, and believe it or not, He just showed me a way out."

"I understand, son," Andrews said. "You wouldn't believe how I understand. But go ahead. Tell me what you have."

"One of the tellers, Kari, Kari Pendelton, has been teaching me sign language," Stephen explained. "She's in here, too. I can use that sign language to give her a message. Then she can talk to John. John's our Security Guard. He used to be in the Navy or something. She is sitting near him. We can make this work."

"Good," said Andrews, recognizing more the advantages of having God on your side. "Go on. Tell me about the people in there. Can we get them all out?"

"There is one lady who is crying a lot," he said. "John will have to usher her out. Then there is an older guy. He looks like he's sleeping but I'm sure he'll be OK. Everybody else should be able to move quickly. I'll go last, make sure everybody else is out."

"Sure you don't want to get out first," Andrews asked. "You're young and fast, right".

"Yes, Sir," Stephen replied. "But I'm the only one in here that knows what's going on. Someone has to show them the way. I have to get them out, Sir."

"You remind me of some folks that I've been talking to over here, son", Andrews said. "OK, let me get everything set up here. I'll let you know when to get the message to them. We don't want to do it too early and get everybody excited. We don't want Lucius in there to catch on that we're up to something."

"Right", Stephen said. "I'll be here."

As Andrews hung up the phone Rivers handed him the other line. "It's Harold Ward, Lieutenant", Rivers said. "Lucius' father."

CHAPTER THIRTY

❧

But Whoever Says
You Fool…

KATHLEEN SULLIVAN WAS STILL ANGRY, STEWING OVER not being allowed into the crime scene.

"Who does that, that Cop, think his is." She spat out Cop like a cobra spewing venom. "That's all he is, a cop. I'm Kathleen Sullivan, a News Reporter. How dare he stand in the way of the press?"

Stewart looked at Kathleen with disbelief in his eyes. She was hissing and sputtering like a snake about to strike.

"I'll show him who I am," Kathleen continued. "I'll have his job. I'm from the news media. When I finish with him he won't be able to get a job as a security guard."

Kathleen turned to look at Stewart. "He can't do that to us, Stu," She said. "He can't keep us out of there."

"Actually, Kathleen", Stu replied nervously, not noticing that he had dropped the endearing Kat, "he can. As long as it's a crime scene, they can keep us out."

"Now what," Kathleen shouted. "You're on his side. You're going to side with that cop. You're from the news also, remember? He kept you out, too. And you're with me. Don't you forget that or I might have to get a new camera man."

Stewart watched Kathleen as she spoke and he once again saw a side of her he had not known. He watched as Kathleen fingered her crystal, rubbing it furiously between her thumb and fingers as if she expected some magic genie to appear. Kathleen's mouth contorted as she spoke, reminding Stewart of the Medusa he had seen in some old movie, hissing and sputtering, the hatred coming from her seeming almost alive, as if she could kill, turn men to stone with a simple glance. He found himself wondering what he had seen in Kathleen. He wasn't so sure he wanted to have that beer with her later. Then Kathleen's visage changed.

"Oh, come on Stu," she cooed. "You know you're my guy. We're a team. It's just that I hate it when those officious morons think that they are better than me. Better than us, Stu."

Kathleen again had that smile on her face. The wind blew her hair just so, the slight breeze causing a strand to flutter in her face, which Kathleen brushed aside with a graceful hand as she turned her head, tossing her hair back into place. The movement caused her perfume to carry on the breeze and waft seductively into Stewarts senses. How beautiful she is, Stewart thought, almost forgetting the Medusa visage. Almost.

"Well," Stewart said as he turned to his camera. "We can't get in and there's nothing we can do about it. Let's find something else to shoot."

"OK," Kathleen chirped as she spun like a little girl headed for the playground. She started towards the main barricade and looked over her shoulder at Stewart, eyes teasingly alive, lips in a pouty smile. "Let's see if we can get a clear shot of the front of the bank from just outside of the barricade."

"She's beautiful," Stewart thought again. "Too bad she has that temper". Stewart noticed she had released her crystal and wondered if it might be causing her mood swings then quickly realized he was being superstitious. Still, he wondered. If those crystals channeled the earth's powers, what powers exactly were being channeled? Shrugging it off, he shouldered his camera and walked off, following Kathleen in pursuit of the news. It was 12:30 in the afternoon. Neither Stewart nor Kathleen saw Fredo Copas standing at the front of the crowds watching the event at the bank unfold, nor would they have known him if they had.

CHAPTER THIRTY ONE

❦

Remember Therefore From Where You Have Fallen…

"Yes, Sir", Andrews spoke into the phone. He had been talking to Harold for about an hour, interviewing him actually. "I'll see that the Chief has all of that information."

"No,' he continued responding to Harold Ward's question. "You stay there. The best place for you to be is at home. We'll know where you are. We can reach you there by phone and you'll be much more comfortable there than being out here."

"Thank you, Sir," Andrews concluded, then hung up the phone.

Andrews turned slowly away from the desk. He looked at the Chief and let out a heavy sigh.

"Not very encouraging, Chief" he said.

"Tell me about it anyway," Samuel said.

"Mister Ward explained to me that Lucius had been a good kid. He had been very proud of him. 'Light of his life', he called him. They were always together, baseball games and such. Lucius loved his father and had always been praising him to his friends. Lately though, Lucius had taken a different turn. He's become rebellious, disobedient. He no longer treated his father as a father but as one beneath his dignity. Lucius recently quit his job because it cut into his partying time. He no longer wants to spend anytime with Mr. Ward, instead running around with a group Ward describes as a bunch of losers. Drugs, alcohol, up at all hours of the night. None of them have a job. They seem to spend all of their time trying to disrupt others. Anything they can do to create trouble."

Andrews paused, looking intently at the Chief before continuing.

"Mister Ward does not believe that Lucius will listen to authority and come out of the bank," he said. "Mister Ward said that he thinks Lucius will kill the hostages thinking it will keep him out of jail, thinking he can defy the authorities. Mister Ward believes that Lucius thinks that he can force everyone to do his will and will do what ever it takes to have his way, even if it means destroying everybody in that bank."

Samuel turned away from Andrews and paced the length of the trailer. After several minutes he finally said as if the conversation had continued uninterrupted, "Still, we have to try. We have to try once more to talk Lucius out before we risk anything else. Let's talk to him one more time."

Andrews could see the pain clearly on the Chief's face. He did not want to lose Lucius. He did not want to lose his son. But he had to save the people. Andrews turned to the desk and reached for the phone. He glanced at the clock on the desk. It was 1:30.

Inside the bank the time was dragging on and the people were becoming weary and restless. Pamela Riesling was looking intently at John. He had his eyes closed but his lips were moving. Pamela figured that he was praying, which made her angry. John was the security guard. He was supposed to be doing something but here he was, with his eyes shut and praying to some god who obviously wasn't paying any attention. If God was paying attention they wouldn't be in this mess in the first place. A god of love would not allow something like this to happen. But it was happening. So there was no God as far as she was concerned.

"John," she whispered hoarsely. "John!"

John opened his eyes and looked towards Pamela. "What are you doing?" she asked.

John glanced over at Lucius who was seated at Pamela's desk. He turned back to Pamela, put a finger to his lips then pointed towards Lucius, indicating that Pamela should remain quiet.

"I will not be quiet," Pamela retorted. "You work for me. Now, what are you going to do about getting us out of here?"

Again John placed his finger to his lips, then with a quick glance at Lucius, John said, "You're going to attract his attention."

Pamela was fuming now. "John, you better do something and you better do it now!"

John looked at Lucius and saw that he was now looking in their direction. John frowned at Pamela and nodded his head towards Lucius. "Quiet," he whispered.

"I don't care about..."the sound of Lucius' chair suddenly moving shocked and quieted Pamela.

"Who's talking over here?" Lucius asked. "Huh, who's talking?" He walked over waving his pistol around, pointing at first one then another of his hostages. John looked at Lucius. Kari averted her eyes and continued praying. Richard Copas looked over at Mary Brown who buried her face in her hands and flopped over to one side, wailing uncontrollably. Pamela froze in fear. Charles McGuire didn't react at all.

"Who's talking?" Lucius said, enjoying the power he had over these people. "Or should I just pick one to shoot?"

"Was it you?" He pointed his gun at Pamela after no one responded. Pamela felt she was going to faint.

"It was me," John said.

Lucius looked at John but continued to keep his gun pointed at Pamela.

"A hero?" he asked. "You want to be a hero?" Lucius glanced at Pamela then looked back at John.

"I heard a woman's voice so I know it wasn't you," Lucius continued.

"But you're brave. I'll give you that. Just like in those old movies. What do they call it, chivalry? She gets to live a little longer for that."

"You should thank him," he said to Pamela who sat frozen in fear not daring to speak.

"I said thank him," Lucius shouted, cocking the hammer on the pistol, which was still pointed at Pamela.

"Thank you, John," Pamela sobbed, tears now rolling freely down her cheeks.

Lucius lowered the pistol and returned to his desk, laughing. As he sat down the phone rang, startling him, causing him to pull the trigger on the cocked pistol. The hammer fell on an empty chamber. Lucius had inserted a full magazine but forgot to feed a round. Quickly he worked the slide on the pistol inserting a round into the chamber, and then carefully lowered the hammer. He wouldn't make the same mistake again.

Lucius then answered the phone. "Hello," he said.

"Lucius, it's Andrews," was the response.

⁓

CHAPTER THIRTY TWO

Sit Here While I Go And Pray…

JACOB PRAYED SILENTLY AS HE PREPARED HIMSELF for the task ahead. He had a job to do, a duty to perform. The people were being held hostage by someone who had no concern, no love, other than for his own pleasure. He had to go get them away from him. He had to set them free. So he went about the physical preparations, making the spiritual preparations at the same time.

"Lord, my precious and holy Father in heaven," Jacob prayed. "I pray Lord that this need not happen. Bring him out so that no one gets hurt. Yet not my will, but Yours be done. Amen."

Kathleen Sullivan was restless, worried. She was angry. She paced back and forth beside the news van parked just outside of the police barricade. Here she was, still the only news crew on this incredible bank robbery. The suspect had taken hostages and she had been able to speak to him. Now she had no further news. Nothing to report. She debated calling Lucius again but decided against it. She had already played that card. She had no more use for Lucius. Now she needed the police to say or do something so she could have something to report, preferably something spectacular. She had her finger on the most important news of the day and here she was, unable to get any closer, unable to speak to anyone, unable to get any more information. The police were ignoring her and that was what made her angry.

"What is going on in there?" Kathleen asked, indicating the police van. "Why won't anyone come out to tell me what is happening? Stu, why won't they talk to me?"

"I don't know Kathleen," Stu answered, shaking his head as he sat lazily with his camera resting on the ground. He was disturbed by her building anger. She seemed to believe that the police couldn't do their job without giving her the play-by-play info. It would be nice to have the news to broadcast but no one owed it to them, as Kathleen seemed to think. The police had their job to do and Kathleen and Stewart had theirs. Kathleen's job was to get the news. Sometimes it didn't just jump into your lap. Sometimes you had to hunt for it. Dig it up. Or wait. Sometimes you had to wait.

"What do you think, Stu?" she asked. "SWAT is here. Do you think they'll barge in there like storm troopers and gun Lucius down? That's the typical police way, isn't it? If they do we'll have it all on film. We'll have the story, won't we?"

"Yes, we will, if they go in," Stu answered. He shuddered at the idea of filming the SWAT team if there was any shooting. He didn't really like the idea of filming anyone dying. Yet Kathleen seemed to relish the idea. Stewart would film it because it was his job. But he hoped he could film the guy surrendering instead.

"That will be great," Kathleen said excitedly. "We can show the footage while I explain how the police went in and gunned down this young man in a hail of gunfire. We'll have the exclusive on it. It will play for days. And I will have the story, Stu. I will have reported it." Kathleen sat in a canvas chair Stewart had set up for her, seeming to calm down. She was holding her crystal again, rubbing it between her thumb and forefinger. As Kathleen continued describing her forthcoming coup Stewart watched her and once again wondered what it was that drove her. Why did she seem to hate the police so much? What was behind her desire to make them look bad all of the time? Stewart was not looking forward to having that beer with Kathleen later.

Suddenly, Kathleen stood up and turned towards Stewart, turning her head sharply to toss her hair out of her face. She smiled broadly revealing teeth beautifully white behind perfect, full lips painted a bright red. Her eyes had a bright shine behind lovely, fluttering lashes. The sunlight reflected off of her thick, stunning hair. "Were going to get this one, Stu," she said. "You and me."

Goodness, she's beautiful, Stewart thought, once again overwhelmed by the vision before him. He smiled and answered, "We'll get it alright."

He looked at his watch. It was 2:00 PM.

Stephen heard the phone ring and peeked through the door. The phone Lucius used was on a desk that was positioned so that when Lucius was on the phone he had to face away from the door to the break room. Stephen was able to look around the bank with little risk of being seen. He looked towards the bank employees. They were all sitting where he had seen them last. No change except that Mrs. Riesling appeared to be crying. Kari was looking in his direction but he was not sure if she could see him. Impulsively, he winked at her. He saw her smile slightly. Stephen put his hand to the gap in the door and slowly, using the signs Kari had taught him, asked if she could see him. Kari nodded her head yes, very slowly. Stephen signed that he would be back soon. Keeping her hands in her lap, Kari signed back, OK. Stephen let the door close. He started thinking of how to sign the message he would have to give soon. He hoped it would be soon. He would have to be fast so he wanted to have it all prepared. He worked out in his mind what he would say and then practiced the signs to say it. There could be no misunderstanding. Lives depended on it. Stephen prayed as he practiced.

As the door closed Kari looked at the others and saw that John had not missed her interaction with Stephen. She smiled at John, wishing she could speak to him, to let him know that she had been praying. That she had come to understand all of the things he and Stephen had been telling her. That it all finally become clear to her, but she was afraid she might agitate Lucius if he heard talking again. "Oh, Lord", she prayed silently. "If only I had the chance to confess Your Name."

John slowly raised his right hand, clenching it in front of his chest, and then started moving his fingers. John signed, "Is he OK?"

Kari was surprised but automatically responded, "Yes. He's up to something."

"God is good," John signed.

"Yes," Kari replied. "And my savior," she told someone for the first time, smiling broadly.

John smiled as he was reminded of an old preacher he had seen at a revival meeting. The preacher made the call to salvation at the end of the meeting, asking those who were accepting Christ as their Lord and Savior to come to the front for the sinner's prayer. As one after another got up from their seats and started to the front of the arena there was polite applause from those in attendance. After several were greeted with this applause the preacher approached the microphone and told a short story. He talked about some men who were watching a football game, The Super Bowl. The score went back and forth and finally in the final few seconds, the men's favorite team was a few points behind with but seconds left on the clock. The center snapped the ball, the quarterback dropped back, found a receiver and threw an impossible pass to the corner of the end zone. The receiver made a jumping fingertip catch landing with both feet just inside the end zone, scoring the game-winning touchdown. What a victory! The men jumped up with a shout and starting hugging each other and slapping high fives all around. They were elated. They had won. Their team was the Super Bowl Champions. They were rejoicing. The preacher then recited from Luke 15:7, "I tell you that in the same way there will be more rejoicing in heaven over one sinner who repents than over ninety-nine righteous persons who do not need to repent." The preacher went on to explain how the angels would rejoice over each person coming to salvation with more joy than those men whose team had won the Super Bowl because it was a greater victory. He then recited the Sinners Prayer with the newly saved souls. As those persons prayed, stating that they accepted Jesus Christ as Lord and Savior, those in the arena let loose with high fives, hugs and shouts of joy for salvation. They were rejoicing. They continued for a brief period, then slowly returned to order.

John's smile broadened as he raised both hands to shoulder level and made the sign for a cheer, then lowered his hands just as Lucius hung up the phone.

CHAPTER THIRTY THREE

≈

But Seek First The Kingdom Of God…

Lt. Andrews hung up after having been on the phone, talking to Lucius, for one half hour. He clasped his hands together and hung his head in defeat. He had tried to reason with Lucius. He had tried to scare Lucius. Lucius refused to listen. Lucius said, again and again, that either the police leave or he would start killing the hostages. When Andrews warned Lucius that the killing of a single hostage would force them to come in after him, Lucius said if the police tried to come in he would kill all of the hostages. Andrews prayed silently for guidance, amazed at how much he had come to rely on prayer so quickly. Then Andrews turned in his seat and looked at the Chief.

"He's not coming out, Chief," Andrews announced. "He said that if we don't leave he'll start killing hostages and if we come in he'll kill them all."

"You've been talking to him, Andy," Samuel said. "Is there anything else we can do?"

Andrews thought for a while then answered, "No, Sir. He's made up his mind. He's made his choice."

"OK," Samuel said, making his decision. "Andrews, get our guy on the inside, Stephen. Alert him so he can start working his plan on the inside. I hope he can make that sign language plan work."

Andrews nodded acknowledgement. Samuel continued, "Someone get Jacob ready. He goes in at three. Any questions?"

There were none. "OK, then", Samuel said. "Let's get those people home."

Vanderhoof looked at Samuel incredulously, still refusing to believe that he would send his son in, that Samuel would rather risk his son's life than risk loosing any of the hostages. What could drive a man to do that? Vanderhoof didn't understand. He just couldn't figure Samuel out. Vanderhoof walked out of the trailer, looking for Jacob.

Andrews picked up the phone they were keeping on an open line to reach Stephen. He asked, "Are you there, Stephen?" There was no answer. He would have to keep trying until Stephen came back to the phone, if he was still able.

Andrews kept the phone to his ear waiting for Stephen to return to the phone. Andrews was getting worried. He hoped that Stephen hadn't been found out. He debated calling Lucius to see if he had been. He kept putting it off afraid that he might arouse Lucius suspicions and get Stephen caught, if he hadn't been already. It was 2:30 and thinking that he had no choice, Andrews was about to put down the phone and call Lucius when he heard the phone being picked up.

"Anybody there," asked Stephen.

"Yes," Andrews answered, relieved. "I've been waiting on you. I was starting to get worried."

"Sorry. I was getting ready on this end," Stephen replied.

"Good," Andrews said. "Are you all set in there, then?"

"I just have to let Kari know what the plan is," he said. "Then we should be ready."

"OK. This is the plan," Andrews started in. "At 3:00 an Officer is going to come to the front of the bank. We hope Lucius will get some sense and decide to come out. If he does, if Lucius comes out, wait until he is in custody. When Lucius is handcuffed then you all come out through the front door, one by one. Got that?"

"Sure," Stephen said. "What if he doesn't go out?"

"That's the hard part," Andrews said. "If he doesn't come out we are going to have to engage with him. Take him out, if we have to. If so, when the shooting starts, I need you to get everybody out of the back door as fast as possible."

"I can do that," Stephen said.

"Turn left once you are outside and have them keep going until they reach the police trailer. Some officers should meet you on the way. Got that? They'll meet you but don't stop until you reach the police trailer."

"Out the back door, left and keep going until we are at the police trailer. Got it," Stephen said.

"Good, "Andrews continued. "But remember. It has to be fast. As soon as we engage Lucius you need to get them moving. You have to get out of there fast. Don't delay. Any hesitation and Lucius has a chance to turn towards you guys and start shooting at you. He will probably try anyway, so you have to get out before he thinks about it. OK?"

"This will be at 3:00," Stephen asked.

"At 3:00," Andrews answered.

"We'll be fast," Stephen said.

Stephen went back to the door and opened it very slowly just wide enough to see into the bank. He could see everyone except Lucius, but he could hear him walking around the bank muttering to himself. He gauged that Lucius would not be able to see the door from where he was so he decided to try to communicate with Kari again. He had the information he had been practicing. Now he hoped he could communicate the actual plan.

Kathleen was sitting staring at the police trailer hoping for some type of news when she saw Vanderhoof leave the trailer quickly. Vanderhoof approached the Chief's son, what was his name? Jacob? Yes, that was it. They had a short conversation then Vanderhoof returned to the trailer. He met Chief Crue at the trailer door where they had a short conversation. Crue then left the trailer and walked over to his son. Vanderhoof watched them for a short while and then entered the trailer, leaving father and son alone. Something's up, thought Kathleen. They're up to something. I don't know what but they're up to something. I'll have to keep watch so I don't miss it. Maybe I can get Stuart to catch something good on video so we'll be ready for the five o'clock news. Kathleen was rubbing her crystal again. She felt good. The crystal would help her find the right news. It always did. It always helped.

Lucius paced back and forth near the desks. He stopped for a second to stare at the hostages. His hostages. "Bunch of big shots came in the bank for money," he thought. "Well, they don't look like such big shots now." They were all under his control. They belonged to him. He didn't care about the police. The police couldn't touch him. He had the hostages. The police had to do what he said. And if they didn't, well, they would as soon as he started shooting hostages. And if the police didn't back off soon, he was going to have to start.

Lucius looked at the hostages again. Which one should go first, he wondered. The security guard? Then he wouldn't have to worry about him again. Still, the guard hadn't tried to do anything, yet. Except take the blame for that lady talking. Some kind of a hero maybe. Maybe he would be first, or better, second. That lady, the one who answered the phone, the one who was doing the talking earlier, maybe she was the president of the bank or something. She should go first. Yes. That would show the police he was serious.

Pamela saw Lucius staring at her and started crying again. She was afraid. Afraid of Lucius. Afraid of dying. Afraid of loosing her job. She couldn't lose her job. She had no control over this. It wasn't her fault. But she was the manager. She was responsible for all of the employees and customers, wasn't she? If someone got hurt it would be her responsibility. Maybe she could give Lucius some money, all of the money, and he would leave. She could talk him into that, she thought. Just take the money and run out real fast. He was young. Maybe the cops couldn't keep up with him. But she couldn't give away the banks money. They would fire her for sure.

But, wait. They couldn't fire her. She was responsible for the daily operation of the bank. This wasn't her job. This was John's job. Why didn't John do something? It was his job to protect the bank. John should do something.

She noticed that Lucius was still staring at her. She was afraid of Lucius. She wanted to scream. Pamela pulled her legs up to her chest, wrapped her arms around them, then put her head on her knees and began to cry in earnest. I can't lose my job, she thought. I can't lose my job.

Mary Brown sat with her left shoulder against the wall, almost lying down. Her knees were drawn up, her face was against the wall. She sobbed incessantly in despair. Her whole world was coming down around her. She should have made the house payment earlier, she thought. But she didn't have the money. She had to wait. Today was the last day to get the payment in on time and finally she had the money. She had to come to the bank to make the payment so that Roger wouldn't find out. Roger would get mad. Now, she was going to be home late. There would be no dinner. She would have to explain to Roger where she had been. Why she had been there. She would have to tell him that his paycheck wasn't enough to pay the mortgage. That she had to wait for his second check. That she had to make the trip to the bank on the bus because they had only one car. Roger was going to be mad. And dinner would not be ready. She didn't like for Roger to be mad. Mary felt totally lost. She had absolutely no hope. She cried. Roger was going to be mad.

Richard Copas sat with his back to the wall, staring blankly into the bank. He wondered where Fredo was. What he was doing. Probably getting drunk again, Richard thought. Probably doesn't even know what's happening here at the bank. What's he going to do when I'm gone, thought Richard. Then the thought entered his mind that his end could come a lot sooner than anyone had thought. Richard looked at Lucius and thought it might happen today. What would Fredo do?

Meanwhile Fredo stood at the barricade looking towards the bank. Fredo was thinking about Richard, his Old Man. His father. I have to take better care of him, Richard thought. He shouldn't be in the bank. Not alone anyway. I dumped him off at the bank and left him just to go see about a job. That's not true, he thought. There was no job. We were just going to hang out and drink beer, pretending to look for work. Maybe somebody would pick one of us for a few hours of work. A gardening job or something. Earn enough for tomorrow's beer. I have to take care of the Old Man. Maybe if I quit drinking and get a job, I can get a job if I quit drinking, then, maybe, I can rent my old room. That will help Pops. Plus I'll have a decent place to live. And I can look after him. But how do I stop drinking. I like hanging out and having a buzz. How do I stop?

"Follow Me", Fredo heard, the voice so close it startled him. Fredo turned quickly expecting to see a police officer standing behind him. In trouble again, Fredo thought, wondering if he was not supposed to be so close to the barricade. The lone officer, Boyarski, was still where he had been when Fredo arrived, standing in the shade near one end of the barricade. "Follow Me," the voice echoed in Fredo's head. "Follow Me." Fredo looked around, trying to find the source of the voice. No one was even paying attention to him. Fredo saw a small church across the street. Not one of the huge ornate ones he had been in before. Just a small, nondescript building with a small sign in front proclaiming, "GODS HOUSE". Everyone welcome, it said. A man stood at the front door, a broom in his hand, watching the activity at the bank. "Follow Me," Fredo heard. He walked across the street.

"Hello," the man said. He was an older man, in his seventies. Yet his voice was strong and confident. "How are you?"

"My father's in the bank," Fredo said, not knowing why he was telling this stranger.

"Let's pray for him," the man said, laying his hands on Fredo's shoulders as if he and Fredo had known each other for years. The man bowed his head and prayed for Richards's safety as well as for the safety of everyone in the bank. "Your will be done," the man closed the prayer. "Amen."

"Amen," Fredo said. The prayer was different, not like anything Fredo had heard before. The man didn't recite endless memorized verses. He, what did he do? He spoke. Like he was talking to someone. He said words. He called God's name and asked Him to hear the prayer. Then he talked, like he was talking to an old friend, an old friend that he respected very, very much.

"Thank you," Fredo said.

"You're looking for something," the man said. It wasn't a question.

"I was late getting my Dad to the bank because I was out drinking late last night," Fredo said. "Then I dropped him of at the bank and left him so I could go drinking again." Fredo couldn't understand why he was talking to this man, telling him his personal business.

"I need to stop drinking," Fredo said. "But I don't know how."

"I know what you need," the man said and motioned for Frodo to follow him inside. Fredo followed. The man entered the sanctuary and sat in the rear pew picking up a well-used bible that was lying on the seat. The man lovingly opened the bible to the book of Matthew and rapidly, jumping from page to page, verse to verse, began preaching Jesus to Fredo. The man then went to the book of John and continued, explaining salvation.

Upon finishing he looked at Fredo and asked, "Did you find what you were looking for?"

Frodo looked at the man, awed by what he had heard. He had sat in church before and listened to priests read from the bible. But no one had ever told him what he heard today. No one had explained the bible to him. Today he heard the word. He heard it very briefly, but what he heard made sense. He heard the truth.

"Yes," Fredo replied breathlessly. "I found it. How do I get it?"

The man led Fredo in the Sinner's Prayer. Fredo accepted the Lord Jesus Christ as his personal savior. He sat and wept. He wept over all of the years he had wasted. All of the years he spent away from the Lord. He also wept over a newfound joy that he felt in his heart. He felt a new life inside himself. He felt strength. Mostly he felt peace. He knew he didn't deserve what ever it was that was in him but he had it now and he was going to hang on to it. At that instant he understood what the man had been telling him. That Jesus loved him, loved him just like he was. He found that he loved Jesus for loving him.

Fredo smiled and stood, whipping away the tears. "Are you the priest here," Fredo asked.

"You mean the Pastor," the man volunteered. "No. I just come in to sweep the place out when I have a chance. And we're having a service tonight, so here I am."

"Oh," Fredo responded. "Then how did you know all of that stuff about the bible?"

"Start reading yours," the man said. "Soon you'll be leading people to Christ also. I have to finish sweeping. And your father's waiting."

The man grabbed his broom and started sweeping a pile of dust that had apparently been left from earlier. The man started praying again, as he swept. It sounded as if he were talking to someone in the room. He thanked his unseen companion for the opportunity to serve. For the chance to share the gospel. For the opportunity to sweep. He gave special thanks for the new member of the family of Christ. Fredo left the church and returned to the barricades. He was talking to his unseen companion as he walked, asking for wisdom, knowledge and understanding. He also asked that his father would be saved. It was 2:45.

Charles Watson McGuire opened his eyes. His collar was soaked with sweat and he felt his back wet under his jacket although the air conditioner was working in the building. He had been sitting on the floor with his back against the wall keeping his eyes closed, pretending to sleep. He was trying to keep himself calm as he imagined his whole world falling down around him. He had been gone for hours. His partners must be missing him by now. If they hadn't noticed that he was missing, Janet, his secretary would be worried and might have gone to them. They would wonder where he had gone. They might think he had gone senile. They would question him when he got back. What excuse could he give for being in the bank? Maybe he could stick to the buying a gift lie. He could say he went to the bank to get some cash for the gift. Why not use a credit card? Why not have Janet get the gift, as usual. Oh, he was going to have to come up with a good story. This robber didn't know that he might be ruining a life here. Years of building a business and this robber's selfish attempt to get some money might ruin Charles. What narcissism. Why do people think that they can take from others for their own gain? What makes these people tick? Now he had to come up with some story so his partners wouldn't find out what he had been up to. Then there was that. That opportunity was gone. He could have made a bundle.

Chapter Thirty Four

❧

Behold, the Hour is At Hand…

STEPHEN STOOD AT THE DOOR, LISTENING, TRYING TO determine where Lucius was. He needed to open the door this one last time to get the information to Kari and he didn't want to get caught. He could hear what sounded like someone walking on the east side of the bank. That would be Lucius and he couldn't see the door from there. Slowly, Stephen pushed the door open ever so slightly. He scanned the bank. He could not see Lucius. Everyone else was still in the same place, having no place else to go. Kari was looking at him as if she had been waiting for the door to open. John was looking at Mrs. Riesling who had her head on her knees. She appeared to be crying.

Stephen winked at Kari, trying to appear brave, although he was scared. But he had to be brave. He couldn't fail. He signed to Kari asking if she could see him. She signed that she could. Slowly, meticulously, Stephen signed that a Policeman would be coming to the bank to save them at 3:00. If Lucius surrendered they would wait in the bank until the police had him in custody. They were then to leave the bank, one at a time, until everybody was out. Kari signed that she understood.

Stephen continued, explaining that if Lucius didn't surrender, they would all have to run out of the bank through the back doors.

"How are we going to do that?" Kari signed.

Stephen signed, "There will be a signal", he didn't want to mention that the signal would be shooting. "At the signal I'll come out. When I do, we have to get everybody moving fast and out through the back door. We stop for nothing."

"OK," Kari signed. "At your signal."

"Once we're out of the bank, turn left and keep running until we reach the police trailer," Stephen explained.

Kari signed back, "Left until we reach the police."

"Left and keep going until we reach the police trailer," Stephen corrected. "Officers will meet us on the way but we keep going until we reach the trailer."

Kari nodded her head, signaling her understanding.

"Can you get the info to John," Stephen signed.

"He's listening," Kari responded.

Stephen looked at John. "Good work," John signed.

Stephen said a quick prayer of praise and thanks to the Lord. Stephen continued the plan. Kari would usher Mrs. Riesling out. John would get the man in the suit, who none of them knew was Charles McGuire. Stephen would come in and get Mrs. Brown and Mr. Copas. Stephen would bring up the rear.

John thought it was probably his job to bring up the rear but his years of military service taught him not to argue the plan at the last minute. He did not know what plans Stephen had arranged so his job now was to carry out his part of the plan. He and Kari signed acknowledgement. They were ready to go.

Stephen signaled that the officer would arrive at 3:00, then closed the door. John checked his watch. It was 2:55. Feeling that familiar, but almost forgotten, feeling that preceded each engagement during his Navy days, John closed his eyes and prayed for calmness, courage and dedication to his mission. And for God's guidance and protection on everyone involved.

Jacob stood behind the police trailer as physically prepared as he could be. He had all of the necessary equipment. He had discussed the plan with Vanderhoof. Only one thing he needed to do now.

Jacob found his father, Chief Samuel Crue. "No other way to do this?" he asked.

"No," Samuel said. "Not if we want to get those people out safely."

"We have to save them," Jacob said.

"Yes, we do, son," Samuel said.

Jacob smiled. "Let's go, then." It was 3:00.

Jacob started walking towards the bank. "Lord," he prayed. Into your hands I commit myself."

Andrews called the bank. Lucius answered.

"Lucius," he said. "An officer is coming to the front of the bank. Talk to him."

"I'm not talking to anybody", Lucius yelled into the phone. "Keep him away."

"Just talk to him," Andrews pleaded.

"If I see a cop I'm going to shoot him then I'm shooting everyone in here," Lucius screamed.

Lucius turned towards the front of the bank and saw Jacob approaching the front doors. He was in a sudden rage. A rage because the police did not do what he wanted. He had hostages and they were not doing what he wanted. Lucius charged towards the front doors, yelling for Jacob to go away.

At the sound of Lucius yelling, Stephen peeked out of the door. He saw Lucius start moving towards the front door. He saw a lone policeman walking towards the door. Stephen was surprised. He expected to see some burley, grizzled SWAT officer armed with the latest weapons. Instead here was a young officer in a blue dress uniform, his pistol still in his holster, approaching the bank. Stephen saw Lucius raise his machine gun.

"Go away," Lucius yelled as he ran to the door. "Go away or I'll shoot everybody."

Stephen burst out of the doors into the bank. As he ran in he saw Kari getting to her feet and moving towards Pamela Riesling. John, moving quick for his age, was half way to McGuire. Stephen tried to pull Mary Brown to her feet at the same time he told Richard Copas to run out of the back doors. Mary started to fall back to the ground, collapsing in her fear. John was trying to get McGuire to his feet but McGuire's bulk was preventing him from moving fast enough. Kari meanwhile, had Pamela up and moving but Pamela stopped, insisting on knowing what was going on.

Suddenly the sound of gunfire erupted in the bank. Richard grabbed Mary and threw her arm around his neck then started running for the back door. Stephen grabbed the back of McGuire's pants as he was trying to crawl to his feet. One good shove and McGuire was up with John shoving him. Richard and Mary ran into Kari and Pamela. Kari, using all of the strength she had, grabbed the protesting Pamela's hand and pulled her towards the back doors. Finally the whole group was moving and picking up speed.

"Run," Stephen shouted. "Run."

Run they did. Out through the rear bank doors with Kari in the lead. Kari was muttering a prayer under her breath as she ran. "Help us, Lord. Help us."

Out of the doors and Kari turned left. Still running and pulling Pamela who was no longer protesting but running for all she was worth.

At the sound of gunfire, Mary Brown came back to life and started running. Seeing that they were heading for the exit doors she redoubled her efforts, now running ahead of Richard. Out of the bank doors and left, following Kari and Pamela. Richard was right behind, but losing ground. Out the doors and left he went.

McGuire waddled close behind Richard, puffing as he moved, starting to tire already. McGuire made a vow to some unknown god to give up cigars and loose weight if he could get out of here safely. Out the door and left, with John right behind, his left hand on McGuire's back, pushing him to an even faster pace.

Stephen came last, following John at what he felt was a casual walking pace. The sounds of gunfire continued as he prayed for those in front of him to move faster. They had already taken too long, much too long. Stephen expected to feel the bullets hitting his back at any second. Miraculously he reached the door. Out the door, left and he was still running. Up ahead he could see Kari running past an officer, then suddenly stop as Pamela stopped at the officer. Kari pulled Pamela as the officer yelled at Pamela to keep running. The whole group kept running. As Stephen ran past the officer he could see the intensity on his face as he crouched in the shadows, his handgun pointing at the back doors of the bank, expecting Lucius to come running out firing his guns. They were out of the bank but still had some running to do before they were safe, Stephen thought, as the sound of gunfire stopped. They finally reached the police trailer. They reached safety. It was 3:01. Barely a minute had elapsed. It seemed an hour.

Chapter Thirty Five

❧

In This Is Love…

IT WAS 4:00. THE POLICE OFFICERS HAD FINISHED their preliminary interviews with the former hostages. They all now stood outside of the police trailer. Kari stood with Stephen, who had draped his jacket over her shoulders. Stephen's arm was comfortably wrapped around her shoulders, also. Kari had already told Stephen about her salvation. John was trying to calm Pamela who was worried about what was happening at the bank. Mary Brown stood off by herself, still crying, wringing her hands. Richard Copas stood looking out towards the street wondering where Fredo was. Charles Watson McGuire was still trying to formulate an explanation for being at the bank.

Chief Crue walked out of the police trailer and over to the group of former hostages.

"When can we go, Chief," Mary asked. "My husband will be worried about me. I have to get home now."

At the same time Charles McGuire said, "I have to get back to my business, Chief. I've been gone much too long. Unless there is any further need of my presence can I get one of your officers to give me a lift back?"

Pamela Riesling asked simultaneously, "What about my bank? When can I get back in there? We've lost a whole day already. I've got to get the bank running again."

Richard continued to stare into the distance, worrying about Fredo.

"Relax, folks. Please relax." The Chief said. "Mr. McGuire. We've called your secretary. She forgot you were gone. She says your partners are out for the day but she sent someone down here to pick you up." He pointed to a security guard who had apparently come from McGuire's building.

Mumbling a quick "Thanks," McGuire walked towards the guard thinking he may have lucked out and escaped this one. If no one was looking for him he didn't have any explaining to do.

"Mrs. Brown," he added. "Your husband called us when he saw what was going on. Apparently he expected you to be at the bank today. He's here for you." Samuel pointed to a large, muscular man standing near the security guard. It was Roger. Mary's heart sank. Roger rushed over to Mary and took her in his arms, holding her close.

"Are you alright Mary," he asked. "Are you alright?" He held her tight, burying her face in his massive chest, stroking her hair, tears flowing from his eyes. Mary was afraid that he would suffocate her and continued crying as they walked away.

"Mr. Copas," the Chief continued. "Your son is right here. He was out at the barricades watching. When he saw people come out of the bank he told our officers who he was. So here he is."

Fredo came over and gave Richard a hug like Richard had not received since Fredo was a little boy. They stood there for a long while, Fredo holding his father.

"Mrs. Riesling," Samuel said. "We were able to contact your husband. He is picking up your children and will be here as soon as he can."

Pamela realized that she hadn't thought once about her family during this whole ordeal. She couldn't she rationalized. She had her work to do.

"Could we have him take the children home," Pamela asked. "I have to finish up here at the bank and they'll just be in the way."

"Does he have a cell phone," Samuel asked. "You can use a phone in here to contact him. Rivers, could you help Mrs. Riesling."

Rivers, who had followed the Chief out of the trailer, led Pamela into the trailer and directed her to the bank of phones.

Meanwhile, on television sets across the state, Channel 3 On The Spot News was interrupting programming with breaking news. The familiar jingle filled the air as the On The Spot News was projected on the screen with a banner reading "Breaking News" superimposed over it. The screen faded to the familiar faces of co-anchors Michael Hale and Caryn Dirkes-DiSalvo.

"We've been following the events at the robbery at the Greater Metropolitan Federal Bank on Center Street," started Hale.

"Yes," continued Dirkes-DiSalvo, "and our own Kathleen Johnson in on the spot with this breaking report."

The screen faded to Kathleen, standing closer to the bank, inside the barricade now. Behind her could be seen yellow crime scene tape cordoning off the front of the bank. Several officers, some in uniform, others in suits, were moving about the area. A Paramedic ambulance was parked directly in front of the bank, partially blocking the view of the bank itself, but adding a certain ambiance to the report.

"Michael, Caryn," Kathleen started. "We reported earlier that a young man, Lucius Ward, had taken hostages in the bank during a foiled robbery attempt. Lucius, denied money by his father attempted to serve his needs by robbing a bank. Lucius had threatened to kill all of the hostages but as far as we could see, he made no attempt to carry out that threat. At three o'clock this afternoon, Police Chief Samuel Crue sent a lone police officer to the front of the bank where this officer gunned down Lucius Ward in a hail of bullets . . .

Suddenly the scene on the screen changed from the beautiful face of Kathleen Johnson to the surrounding area and the sidewalk as the camera was abruptly moved from Kathleen. The screen went momentarily dark then returned to Michael Hale and Caryn Dirkes-DiSalvo sitting in the sanitary newsroom.

"We are having some technical difficulties and have lost our feed," Hale explained. "We'll go to these brief words then return with more as soon as we can get Kathleen back on line."

Michael and Caryn sat with fixed smiles on their faces and pretended to busy themselves with sheets of paper on their desks. The scene changed and a loud obnoxious man appeared on the screen in a commercial add for a mortgage company.

In front of the bank Kathleen had started her report intending to finish in a tirade on how the police had murdered this innocent bank robber without giving him a chance to surrender. Kathleen and Stewart had been allowed near the police trailer after the hostages had been rescued. Unable to speak to the Chief, Kathleen had interviewed Lt. Andrews who explained to her how the Chief's son had sacrificed his life to save the hostages. He explained how there were no other options. It made sense to Stewart, except for the sacrifice. He was still pondering that.

Kathleen asked several pointed questions and smiled a lot then she thanked Andrews for the information. She immediately took Stewart in search of the perfect place to broadcast. They would be live.

After not being allowed past the yellow tape in front of the bank, Kathleen's went into her now customary attempt to belittle everyone who did not bend to her wishes. Losing another round she found the next best place to make her report. Hearing her start to slant the report to the evils that the police had done, Stewart tired of Kathleen. He made a decision that might cost him his job. He made a decision that he was no longer going to be a part of Kathleen fabricating her own truth and reporting it as fact. Stewart lowered his camera as Kathleen was reporting live, then switched it off and walked away. He could hear Kathleen behind him.

"Stewart," she yelled. "Where are you going? We're live. I was reporting."

"Stewart," she continued, not liking being ignored. Then she let loose a tirade of profanity designed to question Stewart's journalistic abilities, his manhood and his ability to identify both of his parents.

Stewart walked over to the police trailer. Seeing the Chief talking with the hostages he started filming what he saw there. Stewart filmed Charles Watson McGuire and Mary Brown being reunited with their people and leaving, failing to thank the Chief for his sacrifice in saving their lives. He filmed Pamela Riesling, who was more concerned with the well being of her business career than with that of her family. He filmed Fredo and Richard and the love of a son for his father. Then he filmed as Kari Pendleton, Stephen Walsh and John Nelson approached the Chief.

"That was your son?" John asked.

"Yes," Samuel answered.

"He died to save us?" Kari asked.

"Yes," Samuel stated.

"Thank you," Stephen said.

Stewart turned off his camera and walked towards the Chief. Stewart said, "I don't understand Chief. How could you sacrifice you son for people that don't even know you?"

The End